# THE BOBBSEY TWINS
# IN RAINBOW VALLEY

# THE BOBBSEY TWINS BOOKS
## By Laura Lee Hope

———————

THE BOBBSEY TWINS
  OF LAKEPORT
ADVENTURE IN THE
  COUNTRY
THE SECRET AT THE
  SEASHORE
MYSTERY AT SCHOOL
AND THE MYSTERY AT
  SNOW LODGE
ON A HOUSEBOAT
MYSTERY AT
  MEADOWBROOK
BIG ADVENTURE AT
  HOME
SEARCH IN THE GREAT
  CITY
ON BLUEBERRY ISLAND
ADVENTURE IN
  WASHINGTON
AND THE COUNTY FAIR
  MYSTERY
CAMPING OUT
WONDERFUL WINTER
  SECRET

AND THE CIRCUS
  SURPRISE
SOLVE A MYSTERY
IN THE LAND OF COTTON
AT MYSTERY MANSION
IN TULIP LAND
IN RAINBOW VALLEY
OWN LITTLE RAILROAD
AT WHITESAIL HARBOR
AND THE HORSESHOE
  RIDDLE
AT BIG BEAR POND
ON A BICYCLE TRIP
OWN LITTLE FERRYBOAT
AT PILGRIM ROCK
FOREST ADVENTURE
AT LONDON TOWER
IN THE MYSTERY CAVE
IN VOLCANO LAND
THE GOLDFISH MYSTERY
AND THE BIG RIVER
  MYSTERY
AND THE GREEK HAT
  MYSTERY

"Up, Kate!" Nan cried suddenly to the bear

*The Bobbsey Twins in Rainbow Valley*

# The Bobbsey Twins
# in Rainbow Valley

*By*

LAURA LEE HOPE

GROSSET & DUNLAP
*Publishers      New York*

*The Bobbsey Twins in Rainbow Valley*

# CONTENTS

| CHAPTER | | PAGE |
|---|---|---|
| I | A FRISKY HUNTING DOG | 1 |
| II | A RUNAWAY MOTORBOAT | 10 |
| III | THE FRIENDLY WOODSMAN | 17 |
| IV | LOG ROLLING | 24 |
| V | THE TURTLE GOES ALONG | 32 |
| VI | THE PLAYFUL RAINBOW | 40 |
| VII | NAN'S STRANGE PET | 47 |
| VIII | THE SINGING WATERFALL | 54 |
| IX | FLOSSIE'S TREASURE | 61 |
| X | THE MYSTERY MAN | 69 |
| XI | BERT'S SEARCH | 76 |
| XII | THE BALLOON MAN | 83 |
| XIII | LITTLE HOOTY | 91 |
| XIV | A MEAN TRICK | 99 |
| XV | THE RESCUE BEAR | 105 |
| XVI | CAPTAIN BOBBSEY | 112 |
| XVII | FREDDIE IN A RACE | 119 |

| CHAPTER | | PAGE |
|---|---|---|
| XVIII | TWIN DETECTIVES . . . . | 127 |
| XIX | THE INDIAN TRAIL . . . . | 134 |
| XX | THE HELPFUL "ICICLE" . . . | 142 |
| XXI | THE OLD CABIN . . . . . | 147 |
| XXII | ALONE IN THE WOODS . . . | 152 |
| XXIII | A SURPRISE . . . . . . | 160 |
| XXIV | THE SECRET PATH . . . . | 165 |
| XXV | HAPPY CHILDREN . . . . | 173 |

# CHAPTER I

### A FRISKY HUNTING DOG

"OH DEAR," Flossie Bobbsey said, "there's nothing here but milk and eggs and—"

"Here, let me take a look," her twin brother Freddie offered. "We just *have* to have some raw meat for our drag."

Freddie and Flossie Bobbsey, six years old, were standing in front of the refrigerator in their kitchen. The big white door was wide open, and Flossie's blonde head was poked inside. Suddenly a voice from behind them made the twins jump.

"My goodness! Why you lettin' so much warm air in the icebox?"

Dinah, the stout, kindly Negro cook who worked for the Bobbsey family, walked up and shut the door.

"Please help us with our drag, Dinah," Freddie said. "We need some raw meat to make one."

Dinah had lived in the South and knew that a

drag was something you pulled along the ground to leave a scent for a dog to follow.

"Where'd you children hear about a drag?" Dinah asked.

"Daddy told us," Freddie replied. "He says that's the way they train hunting dogs. I'm going to be a dog trainer!"

"We want to put our dog Waggo in the Sportsman's Show," Flossie added. "It's coming to Lakeport tomorrow."

Dinah shook her head doubtfully. "That's not much time to train a huntin' dog," she said.

"Waggo's very smart," said Flossie. "We want him to win a prize."

The little girl told Dinah that they were looking for a piece of meat to drag along the ground. After Waggo, their fox terrier, had sniffed the scent and found the meat, Flossie said, he would be a hunting dog and they could enter him in the show.

Dinah chuckled. She reached far back into the refrigerator and pulled out a big piece of stew meat. She tied a string to it.

"Here's your drag," she said, smiling. "When you make a huntin' dog out of Waggo, make him hunt up a rabbit for me!"

"Thank you, Dinah," the twins said, and dashed out into the yard.

Waggo was lying in the sun by his doghouse. He stood up and barked when he heard the children. Freddie held the meat behind his back so the dog could not see it.

"We'll have to blindfold Waggo," the little boy said, "till we hide the drag."

Flossie thought this was a good idea. She took a handkerchief from her pocket and tied it over Waggo's eyes.

"Quiet, Waggo!" she ordered when the dog wiggled. "We're going to play a game."

Freddie dropped the meat on the ground and dragged it by the string around the yard. Then he zigzagged through the back yards near the Bobbseys' house, and through the fields, until he came to the brook. He put the meat on top of a stump and raced back to Flossie.

"Let Waggo go!" he cried.

Flossie untied the blindfold. Waggo sniffed the ground and wagged his tail very fast. Then he barked as if to say, "This is a good game!"

He started running excitedly along the trail Freddie had laid. The children raced behind him.

"Waggo's a hunting dog already!" Freddie shouted.

Hardly had he said this when Waggo stopped hort.

"Oh, look!" Flossie exclaimed in a frightened tone. "He sees a cat!"

"He won't chase her," Freddie said stoutly. "Waggo's a hunting dog. He won't give up the trail."

But Waggo did give up the trail. He yelped and dashed after the cat, which ran up a tree trunk. Waggo stood barking at the bottom of the tree until Freddie pulled him away.

"You'll never win a prize that way," the little boy scolded.

Waggo seemed to understand this time, and soon picked up the scent again. He kept on the trail for a few minutes and then dashed among some bushes.

"Oh dear," Flossie sighed, "we'll never make a hunting dog out of him."

The twins could see his tail wagging under the bushes. The dog made loud sniffing noises.

"Maybe he's found something," Freddie defended his pet. "A hunting dog can hunt for anything."

Half a minute later Waggo backed out with an old baseball glove in his mouth. He dropped it at Freddie's feet.

"This is no good, Waggo," the little boy said. "You ought to—" Freddie had put his hand into the glove. He pulled out a shiny nickel! "Say, you're a good hunter after all, Waggo," Freddie exclaimed.

Waggo wagged his tail happily and picked up the trail again. He scampered to the stump beside the brook. Here he stopped and stood barking. Freddie and Flossie ran to the spot. The meat was gone!

"Somebody took Waggo's meat!" Freddie cried.

While the twins were trying to figure out who could have taken it, Bert and Nan, their older brother and sister, came along. Bert and Nan were twins also. They were twelve years old and looked different from Flossie and Freddie. The little Bobbseys had blonde hair and blue eyes. Bert and Nan had dark hair and brown eyes.

Freddie explained how he and Flossie were training Waggo to be a hunting dog, and told about the stolen meat.

"Another dog ran off with it," Nan exclaimed. "He went past us. A big black dog. I never saw him before."

Bert said he thought the dog belonged to Danny Rugg, a boy none of the twins liked.

"Danny's a mean boy to let his dog eat Waggo's meat," Flossie declared. "Never mind, Waggo. Come on home and I'll give you another piece."

On the way, the twins talked about the Sportsman's Show. Bert said that Waggo could not be entered. The kind of hunting dogs they had in shows took a long time to train. A dog had to do more than just follow the scent of a piece of meat.

"Those show dogs have to know how to behave before a lot of people," he said. "They can't run around wild the way Waggo does."

Freddie and Flossie were disappointed that their pet could not be in the Sportsman's Show, but they decided that maybe he had more fun "running around wild" at home.

As the twins reached the house, Mr. Bobbsey turned into the driveway and stepped out of his car. He pulled a white envelope from his pocket and waved it toward the children.

"Here are the tickets for the Sportsman's Show," he said. Lifting Flossie up in his arms, he asked, "What does my Fat Fairy say to that?" Daddy Bobbsey liked to call his little girl by this name. "And my Little Fireman," he added, patting Freddie on the shoulder.

Freddie grinned. "I think it's swell," he answered. "When can we go?"

"Tomorrow morning," said Mr. Bobbsey. "I'm taking the day off."

Flossie hugged her father, then got down. She

wanted to get another piece of meat to give Waggo. But Waggo had disappeared.

"Maybe he went to fight that bad dog," Flossie said, worried. "Bert, please go over to Danny's and see if Waggo's there."

Waggo was not at Danny's house, but Bert learned from Danny's mother that the big black dog did belong to Danny. In a little while Waggo returned home. Flossie examined him carefully to see if he had been in a fight, but he was all right.

Next morning the Bobbsey twins woke up early. Their father, who liked to hunt and fish and camp out in the woods, laughed about their being so prompt for breakfast. No dawdling this morning!

"Take care, children, and don't fall in the lake," Dinah cautioned them as they piled into the car after breakfast. "I don't want you comin' home before you see everything."

"We won't," the twins called.

Mr. Bobbsey headed for the shore of Lake Metoka, where the show was being held. The Bobbseys lived in Lakeport, only a short distance from the lake front.

"I see the Sportsman's Show!" Freddie shouted as they neared the spot. "Gee, it looks swell!"

Large tents had been pitched. Flags were fly-ing from the tops of them. A number of motor-boats were whizzing across the lake.

"Boy, I hope we can ride in one of those boats!" said Bert.

"Later on," his father said. "First, let's see what's inside the tents."

After Mr. Bobbsey parked the car, he led them from one booth to another, looking at the wonderful things that sportsmen like. There were exhibits of fishing tackle. There were lit-tle rowboats which could be folded up and put in the back of an automobile. There were big camping tents and little pup tents.

Suddenly Freddie gave his father's hand a tug. "Daddy, look at the bows and arrows. I want to shoot one. I want to play Indian!"

Mrs. Bobbsey, who was holding Flossie's hand, smiled at her little son. Freddie always wanted to be a fireman or a policeman or whatever else came to his mind at the moment.

"All right," Mr. Bobbsey said. "We'll all play Indian."

"You too, Dad?" Nan asked in surprise.

"Of course. Mother too."

Freddie and Flossie jumped up and down with glee as they approached the long counter on which lay bows and arrows.

"Six tickets," Mr. Bobbsey said. The attendant took the money and told the Bobbseys to help themselves to any sets of bows and arrows they wanted.

"Mother and I will shoot first," said the twins' father. "Watch carefully!"

Mrs. Bobbsey laughed, picked up a bow, strung an arrow and—zip! It hit the bull's-eye! The twins clapped. Mrs. Bobbsey hit the bull's-eye three times out of eight draws. Then Mr. Bobbsey tried. He hit the target five times.

"I'm next," Freddie shouted.

He was so excited that Mr. Bobbsey decided to let him be the next one to shoot. Freddie strung the bow and pulled the string back very carefully. He aimed at the target. But just as he was about to shoot, his fingers slipped off the string.

The arrow flew straight up into the air, then started down.

"It's going to hit that man!" Nan shrieked.

# CHAPTER II

## A RUNAWAY MOTORBOAT

FREDDIE'S arrow fell directly toward a man who was wearing a stiff straw hat. It knocked the hat over his eyes. Startled, the man jumped to one side and his hat fell off.

"Who shot that arrow?" he roared, striding toward the Bobbseys.

He was a tall man with a very thin face and small black eyes. Mr. Bobbsey told him that the arrow had been shot by his young son, and apologized for the accident. Freddie spoke up and said he was sorry.

"If your hat has been damaged," the twins' father offered, "I'll be only too glad to pay for a new one."

The man glared at Freddie. "I don't want a new hat," he growled. "I want that kid spanked."

Mr. Bobbsey said he would do nothing of the sort.

"I ought to spank him myself," the unpleasant man said.

Freddie was worried. He had meant no harm. But things like this often happened to him, and to Flossie and Bert and Nan, too. They were always having adventures of one sort or another.

Only recently they had had a wonderful time in Tulip Land. There they had played with a Dutch boy and girl and solved a little mystery about a stolen book.

Right now Freddie was wondering if the man whose hat he had knocked off would really try to spank him. But Mr. Bobbsey was tall and broad-shouldered, and so the unpleasant stranger only walked off grumbling. The little boy was relieved.

"I guess I'd better help you with the arrows," said Mr. Bobbsey, and held them until Freddie was ready to let go. The little boy actually made a bull's-eye!

Soon it was Bert's turn. He had decided to try to better his father's score of five points. It was not until Mr. Bobbsey had bought three more sets of arrows, though, that the boy managed to hit the center of the target six times in a row.

"You win, son," his father praised him.

"For a prize I'll take a ride in a boat," said Bert, grinning.

His father gave Bert and Nan some money, and they walked down to the shore of the lake.

"There's a dandy boat," Bert exclaimed, pointing to one tied alongside a dock.

He walked out to the end of the dock. Nan followed. Rocking gently in the water was a little red boat with an outboard motor attached to the stern. As the twins admired it, a salesman walked up to Bert. He handed him a pamphlet.

"This will tell you all about it, son," he said, smiling. "The motor is so simple that any kid can operate it."

"You mean I could run it without taking lessons?" Bert asked eagerly.

"Sure thing. Want to try?"

"Oh boy!" Bert cried. "May I take my sister for a ride?"

"Sure," said the salesman.

Nan climbed into the front of the boat while her brother sat down in the stern by the motor. As the salesman was showing Bert how to start and stop it, a boy approached them, frowning.

"Hello, Danny," Nan said. "Isn't this a wonderful boat? Bert and I are going for a ride in it."

"That's the boat I wanted a ride in," Danny said peevishly.

The salesman shook his head. "Only two at a time are allowed to ride in this boat. You can go some other time, sonny."

Danny clenched his fists. He did not like to be disappointed. Furthermore, he did not like the twins to have fun which he could not share.

"I'll bet the Bobbseys told you not to let me have a ride," he snapped at the salesman. Then he stomped off the dock and stood by the edge of the water.

Bert pressed the starter button and the motor purred. The propeller made the water churn and bubble. Just as Bert was about to cast off, Nan cried, "Look out!"

Her brother turned in time to see Danny throw a large rock. It hit the motor with a bang. Danny ran off.

"That boy won't ever get a ride now!" the salesman exclaimed angrily.

He examined the motor. It was still running and appeared to be undamaged. He slipped the rope and shoved the boat off. Bert made the motor go faster. The boat whizzed off up the lake.

"This is fun," Nan cried. The wind whipped through her hair.

Bert grinned. He guided the boat like a real skipper, holding it on a true course. Keeping close to shore, he covered a quarter of a mile. Then he steered the boat around and they hummed back.

"How'd you like to go in circles?" he called to Nan.

"Sure, and fast, too!"

Bert turned around in a big circle. Pretty soon the little motorboat was heading back into the waves which it had made.

Slap, slap, slap! The waves spanked the bottom of the boat. Nan was jounced up and down, and hung onto the sides.

She laughed and said, "Oh, Bert, it's like a roller coaster. Do it again!"

Her twin made another circle. The red motorboat bobbed up and down.

After they had done this several times, Bert decided to see how slow the boat could go. He throttled the motor down until it went *chug-chug—chug—chug*.

Nan leaned over and let her hand trail in the water. A moment later she said, "Ouch! Something bit me!"

Bert swung the boat around to the spot.

"There it is!" his sister shouted.

A few feet from the boat and several inches under water, swam a small turtle.

"I'll try to grab him," said Bert.

He reached out and carefully lifted the turtle from the water.

"He's not a snapper," the boy said, handing the little turtle to Nan.

The turtle stretched its neck and made a paddling motion with its legs.

"We'll keep it to play with," said Nan. "Flossie and Freddie will love the turtle." She examined it closely. "Why, Bert, there are initials on the shell." The letters G. G. had been cut into the turtle's shell.

"I wonder if it belongs to anyone in Lakeport," said Nan. "Let's try to find out."

She put the turtle in the bottom of the boat. It crawled under the seat.

"I think we ought to go back and give other people a chance to ride," Nan suggested.

Bert agreed, and guided the little craft toward the dock. Nearing it, he tried to shut off the motor. It would not stop!

Bert tried again and again, just as the salesman had shown him. Still the motor kept on chugging. The boat was now close to the dock. Bert had to swing it around fast in order to avoid a crash. He looked about excitedly for the salesman, but he was not in sight!

"What's the matter?" Nan asked.

Bert told her, and added, "I'll bet Danny Rugg broke something when he hit the motor."

The boy wondered what he should do. He could keep on going around in circles until the gasoline was used up, but this might take a long time.

A moment later a voice on shore rang out through a megaphone: "All boats ashore! The race starts in three minutes!"

Nan and Bert looked wildly at each other. They could not take the boat ashore! There was only one thing to do—race to the end of the lake ahead of the other boats.

Bert opened the throttle as far as it would go, and headed out into the lake. Everything went well for a minute, then suddenly the motor stopped. Bert tried frantically to start it. No luck!

"We're drifting! A boat will hit us!" Nan cried. "Help! Help!"

# CHAPTER III

## THE FRIENDLY WOODSMAN

THE ONLY person who heard Nan was a tall, elderly man on shore. Without waiting, he jumped into a canoe and shoved off with the paddle.

Never had the twins seen anybody paddle so fast. The canoe fairly zipped through the water. The man knelt in the stern, his arms working rapidly. Each powerful stroke seemed to lift the front of the canoe right out of the water. In no time at all he drew near the two children.

"What's the trouble?" he shouted.

"I can't start the motor," Bert called. "First it wouldn't stop, and now it's dead!"

"Please take us off!" Nan pleaded. "The racing boats are coming!"

The stranger told the twins to hold his canoe steady. He stepped cautiously into the motorboat and tried to start the engine. Still it would not work.

From down the lake came the sound of a pistol shot. The race had started!

"I'll tow you!" said the stranger.

He picked up the loose end of the rope which was tied to the prow of the twins' boat, and stepped cautiously back into his canoe. Quickly he fastened the rope to a crossbar, then started paddling like mad.

At first it was hard work. But in a few moments the motorboat glided slowly after the canoe. The twins reached shore not a moment too soon. Four speedboats roared past them.

"Oh, thank you so much, Mr. . . ." Bert stopped.

"Lincoln. Lincoln's my name."

Nan's mouth dropped open. "You do look like Abraham Lincoln!" she said.

For the first time the twins got a good look at the man. He was much older than their father and had dark wavy hair and a beard that looked like Abraham Lincoln's. His shoulders were broad and his arms were long.

"Are you related to Lincoln?" Nan asked.

Mr. Lincoln smiled. Nan liked his eyes when they crinkled up.

"I'm a woodpile relation, I guess you'd call it," he said. "That's why folks call me Old Abe."

"Do you live around here?" Bert asked. He

had never seen the interesting old man in Lake-port.

"No. I'm a woodsman," Mr. Lincoln said. "I'm only here for the Sportsman's Show. I have an exhibit."

"What is it?" Bert asked.

The woodsman said he sold woven baskets which he had made during the winter. Just then he saw the turtle crawling in the bottom of the boat.

"When did you get him?" he asked. Nan told him. "It's a small world," the old man said. "I put that turtle in Lake Metoka only this morning."

"Was he your pet?" Bert asked.

"Not exactly. He . . ." Mr. Lincoln suddenly stopped. "Here comes the boat salesman," he said.

The salesman had seen the canoe towing the red boat and came running along the shore to find out what had happened. He was thankful the twins were safe. Jumping into the red boat, he began tinkering with the motor. Finally he shook his head and said that a mechanic would have to fix it.

"I know it's not your fault," he said to Bert. "But if I lay my hands on that young scamp who threw the stone . . ."

Bert and Nan thanked the salesman and walked off with Mr. Lincoln to see his exhibit. The twins helped him arrange his woven fishing baskets and picnic kits.

"They're very attractive," said Nan.

At that moment Mr. and Mrs. Bobbsey and the younger twins came along. After hearing about the rescue and thanking Mr. Lincoln, the twins' father bought one of the fishing baskets.

"We can use this at Rainbow Valley," he told the children.

"Rainbow Valley?" the woodsman repeated.

"We're going to spend our vacation there," Mr. Bobbsey answered. "Do you know the place?"

Mr. Lincoln did not reply for a moment. Finally he said, "Why—uh—yes." Then he turned to wait on another customer.

Nan wondered why the old woodsman had acted so strangely about Rainbow Valley. As she was thinking about it, Flossie suddenly spied something at a near-by booth.

"Look!" she cried. "A fish pond."

The pond was a tank about twice as big as a bathtub. In one corner were half a dozen fish.

"Would you like to fish?" asked a man standing near the tank. "No charge. This is a game for small children."

The younger twins said they would like to play. The man handed them two long sticks. These were the fishing poles. A string was attached to each one, and at the end of the string hung a piece of metal.

"That's the bait," the man explained.

"It isn't a worm," Flossie said doubtfully. She had never fished with anything but a worm. "How can a fish eat a piece of iron?"

"You'll see."

The man reached into the pond and pulled out the fish one by one. Flossie's and Freddie's eyes popped. The fish were not alive!

"They're rubber fish!" Freddie exclaimed.

The attendant wound up a key on the side of each fish and put them back into the water.

"Ready!" he said to Freddie and Flossie. "Catch your fish. Put the bait right near their noses."

Flossie giggled. The rubber fish began to move their tails from side to side just like real fish. They swam to and fro across the little pond.

Freddie and Flossie held their poles over the pond and dangled the bait in front of each fish as it came by. Suddenly one seemed to jump toward the little boy's line.

"I've got him!" he cried. But Freddie was so excited that he jerked the bait away too quickly.

"Oh gee," he said, "I lost him."

Another fish came up to Flossie's line. She also pulled too hard and lost it.

"Draw the line in slowly," the man advised. "Your bait is a magnet."

He explained that the rubber fish had little motors inside which made their tails wiggle. In their noses was a tiny piece of iron. Tied to the end of the fishing lines were magnets.

This time Freddie was careful. He dangled the magnet right in front of a wiggling fish, and kept it there. In a moment the fish stuck to the bait.

Freddie laughed happily, then began to pull in his line slowly. The fish stayed on and he lifted it out of the pond.

"Golly, I caught a fish!" he exclaimed.

By this time all the fish had stopped wiggling. The little motors inside their stomachs had run down. They lay still on the water.

Flossie was disappointed. She had not caught a wiggling fish.

"Oh dear," she sighed, "I guess girls can't fish as well as boys."

"Nonsense," Mr. Bobbsey said. "Your mother caught a very big fish when we went camping last year."

Mrs. Bobbsey laughed. She told Flossie that

when she was having no luck, she had said, "Big
fish, please bite my hook." Right afterward she
had caught one.

This gave Flossie an idea. She looked into the
pool and said, "Big fish, please bite my hook."

As if by magic, one of the fish suddenly began
to move his tail. Slowly but surely it headed directly toward Flossie! The little girl reached out
her hand.

"Oh goody!" she exclaimed. "He's coming!"

Indeed, it seemed as if the rubber fish had
heard Flossie's wish. It swam right into her
hand, then stopped wiggling.

"I guess the spring had a few turns left in it,"
the salesman said, laughing.

Flossie had picked up the fish. She put her
nose right to the fish's nose. "You had just
enough wiggles left, didn't you?" she said.

Suddenly Nan grabbed her twin's arm.
"Bert," she said, "we forgot all about the turtle!
He's still in the boat. Somebody might step on
him! Come on!"

# CHAPTER IV

## LOG ROLLING

WHEN Flossie and Freddie heard about the turtle, they started running after Nan and Bert. Mr. Bobbsey sped behind them.

"We'll meet you at the log rolling," he called to Mrs. Bobbsey, who did not like to run so fast.

Fortunately, the mechanic had not come yet to fix the motor, so no one had disturbed the turtle.

"Let me hold it," Freddie begged.

"I wouldn't like to be a turtle," Flossie declared. "He never can get out of his shell."

"But he can go swimming any time," Freddie piped up. "Oh, look, he's got a name."

Since no one knew what the initials G. G. stood for, Flossie called him Gee Gee, and that became the turtle's name.

"Now let's walk down to the log rolling," said Mr. Bobbsey. "I have a surprise for you."

The twins knew quite a lot about log rolling.

Their father was in the lumber business, and once he had taken them to Canada when he went there to buy lumber. Up there, log rolling was part of the work of floating logs down the rivers. Today's log rolling in Lakeport was to be only a contest to see who could stand the longest on a floating log.

"I like it when the men fall off," said Freddie, chuckling.

"It's very hard to stay on a log that's whirling around in the water," Mr. Bobbsey declared.

"Oh, that's what my teacher must have meant!" Flossie exclaimed. "She once said 'rithmetic was easy as falling off a log!"

"That's right," her father said. "The game is to stay on yourself and make the other fellow lose his balance."

"Here they come!" Bert called out.

Several men carried a big log to the lake and rolled it into the water. Two young fellows in plaid shirts, one black and red, one yellow and blue, and dungarees tucked down into high, laced boots, pushed the log from shore, and nimbly hopped on. Then they started rolling the log by making their feet go very fast.

First the log rolled one way. Then it rolled the other way. The two men were waving their arms and dancing up and down as if they were doing a jig.

"I can't understand how they stay on those logs so long!" Nan exclaimed.

A man standing next to her explained that the two men had tiny, sharp nails called brads on the soles of their boots, which helped keep them from slipping off.

Suddenly the man in the blue-and-yellow shirt teetered to one side. He made his legs go very fast to keep his balance, but he fell into the water with a splash. Everybody laughed, and Freddie roared with delight.

As the man swam back to the log and pulled himself onto it again, the Bobbsey twins noticed that their father was no longer there. Mrs. Bobbsey had come up, and Nan asked her where he had gone.

Mrs. Bobbsey's eyes twinkled. "Oh, didn't he tell you about the surprise?"

"No, Mother. What is it?"

"Well, you wait and see."

A moment later the logger in the blue-and-yellow shirt fell off again. The man wearing the black-and-red plaid was declared the winner.

"Now listen carefully," Mrs. Bobbsey said to the children.

The announcer spoke into his microphone.

"Ladies and gentlemen, we have a surprise for you today. Two of our good citizens, who used to do some log rolling as boys, are going to give us an exhibit. No need to introduce either of them."

From a tent walked two men. One of them was Mr. Bobbsey!

"Gee, I never knew Dad could roll logs!" Bert exclaimed proudly.

Mrs. Bobbsey smiled as the twins' father and Dr. Anson, a dentist, wearing swimming trunks and sport shirts, waded into the water and climbed onto the log.

"Two out of three wins," the announcer called through the loud-speaker.

The men started rolling the log. The twins held their breath. Almost at once Dr. Anson pitched into the water. Mr. Bobbsey followed a few seconds later.

"They each have one fall," Mrs. Bobbsey told the twins. "The man who stays on this time wins."

"Daddy!" Freddie screamed. "Beat him!"

The men started rolling very carefully. The log came closer and closer to where Mrs. Bobbsey and the children were standing on the dock. Suddenly their father started treading very fast with his feet.

The log whirled around. The crowd shouted as the men tried to keep their balance. Suddenly Dr. Anson made a funny face.

"He's going to fall!" Bert cried.

The words were hardly out of his mouth when the dentist pitched backward and fell in with a big splash. Mr. Bobbsey teetered and teetered but finally caught his balance.

"Daddy wins! Daddy wins!" Freddie screamed.

While Mr. Bobbsey was changing his clothes, the twins and their mother went back to the fish pond. Several children were playing the game. Finally Freddie and Flossie went to talk to Mr. Lincoln. Since he was not busy just then, the twins asked him many questions about the woods. The old woodsman seemed very glad to answer them.

"Do you have a car with beds in it?" Flossie said. She had seen one on exhibition.

"No, indeed," he replied, laughing. "I live in a cabin."

"But suppose you're out in the woods and it gets dark?" Freddie wanted to know. "What do you do then?"

The woodsman said, "When I sleep in the woods overnight, I make a lean-to."

"What do you lean on?" Flossie asked.

Mr. Lincoln chuckled. "Would you like me to make a lean-to right now?"

"Oh yes, please," the twins begged.

Mr. Lincoln left his booth and walked over to a big pile of branches. They had been lopped off a tree which had been cut down to make room for the Sportsman's Show. From his pocket he took a big penknife and pressed a button on the side of it. A sharp blade popped up.

"This is how you make a lean-to," the old woodsman said.

He picked up a dozen branches and cut them all the same length. Then he took all the small twigs off a very long branch. Next he pulled up a piece of trailing vine.

"Now we're ready," he said.

He carried everything over to two little trees which stood about five steps apart. Using the vine as a cord, he tied the ends of the long pole to the two trees. Next he stood the branches up on a slant against the pole.

"You're making a one-sided house, Mr. Lincoln," Nan guessed, joining her little brother and sister just then.

"That's right. A lean-to comes in handy to keep out the rain on a stormy night."

"Mr. Lincoln, don't you ever get lonesome in the woods?" Flossie asked.

"No," he answered. "I have a pet bear to keep me company. Her name is Kate." He smiled. "When I say, 'Up, Kate!' she stands on her head."

"Oh, I wish I could see Kate stand on her head!" cried Freddie.

A customer came to the basket booth, and Mr. Lincoln turned to wait on her. Mrs. Bobbsey said the children must go home now to eat luncheon and rest, then come back to the show later.

Freddie and Flossie wanted Bert to see the lean-to, so Mr. Lincoln's booth was the first place they went when they got back at four o'clock. To their surprise, the booth was empty and the old woodsman was nowhere in sight.

"Where'd Mr. Lincoln go?" Nan asked the fishing-pond man.

He shrugged. "I didn't notice. Maybe he took his baskets to a better spot."

Bert liked the lean-to. While he was examining it, he spied a penknife on the ground and picked it up.

"That's Mr. Lincoln's," Freddie declared.

The twins set off to find the woodsman, but he was not at any booth in the show. Finally Bert went to the manager.

"I'm afraid I can't help you, son," the man said. "Mr. Lincoln never did talk much, and he left here without saying a word. He seemed to have something on his mind, though."

"I found his penknife and I'd like to return it," Bert told him. "Shall I leave it with you?"

"No," said the manager. "We close down to-night, and I don't want anything on my hands. You keep the knife. If Mr. Lincoln shows up, I'll tell him you have it."

In the meantime, Nan had kept on looking for the nice old woodsman. His knife must be pretty important to him. But she had no better luck than Bert, and finally gave up.

She was on her way to find her twin when she thought she heard the word 'Lincoln.' Rounding the corner of a large booth, she saw two men. They were so busy talking that they did not see Nan. One of them was the unpleasant man whose hat Freddie had knocked off with the arrow.

"I'm sure the man I saw was Old Abe," the man with him was saying. "Listen, Smink, we'd better get moving. They say he has gone to the city."

The unpleasant man nodded. "We mustn't let the old fellow get away with anything."

Suddenly they spied Nan and stopped talk-ing. Had they been referring to nice Mr. Lin-coln? Nan was worried.

# CHAPTER V

## THE TURTLE GOES ALONG

WITHOUT thinking, Nan ran up to the men and asked if they knew where Mr. Lincoln was. They looked at each other in surprise. Then Mr. Smink said, "Run along, little girl, and mind your own business."

"But I *must* find Mr. Lincoln. I—we have something that belongs to him," Nan said, without moving from the spot.

"Give it to me, and if I see him I'll hand it over," Mr. Smink told her.

"I haven't it with me," Nan said aloud. To herself she added, "And if I did, I wouldn't give it to you. I don't like you!"

The men walked off. Nan bit her lip in chagrin, then went to find Bert and the others. When Bert heard the story, he decided to try and find out where Mr. Lincoln came from. This took a long time, but finally Bert had some luck. Thinking the woodsman might have rented the canoe that had brought him to their rescue, he spoke to the boat salesman.

"Yes, Mr. Lincoln did rent the canoe from me," the man said. "He mentioned Westbrook in his conversation. Maybe he's from there."

"Where's Westbrook?" asked Bert.

"Well, it's about a hundred miles from here. It's in Rainbow Valley. Ever hear of that place?"

"Sure," said Bert, "I'm going there in a few days with my family."

The Bobbseys were going to live in a cabin which was one of several owned by a big hotel. Dinah would do the cooking for the family and help look after the younger twins.

"Why do they call it Rainbow Valley?" Flossie asked later, when Bert had returned home with his news.

Nan said her father had told her that a rainbow often appeared over the valley. And there was one rainbow that could be seen there most of the time.

"Where's that?" asked Freddie.

"Down by a waterfall."

His sister said that a beautiful waterfall came thundering down over a cliff and when the sun shone on the foaming water, a lovely rainbow appeared.

Dinah smiled at Freddie and Flossie.

"Maybe you can find the pot o' gold at the end of the rainbow."

Freddie was making Waggo jump through his arms. When he heard what Dinah said, he stopped playing with the dog.

"Is there *really* a pot of gold at the end of the rainbow?" he asked excitedly.

Dinah shrugged. "That's what the old story says," she replied.

Freddie decided at once that he would be a gold miner. It would be more fun than being a log roller.

"I'm going to hunt for the pot of gold," he shouted.

He ran from the house and out to the garage. In a few minutes he returned with a small shovel and the round, red sieve he used when playing in the sand. Freddie once had seen a picture of miners sifting gravel to find gold.

"I'm going to take these with me," he announced, and carried them upstairs to his bedroom so that he would not forget them.

During the next few days the Bobbsey home was buzzing with activity. Vacation clothes were cleaned, new playsuits were bought, and trunks were packed.

Flossie was busy with her dolls. She just could not bear to leave any of them in Lakeport.

Nan and Bert were busy, too. Nan packed a badminton set, while Bert repaired his fishing tackle. Freddie made sure they had the mechanical fish and line his father had bought at the Sportsman's Show.

Soon the big day came. Mr. Bobbsey drove their car out of the garage. The children helped carry the small luggage, which their father packed in the rear compartment. The trunks had been sent ahead, so there was not much to take in the car.

Mr. and Mrs. Bobbsey and Bert sat in front. Dinah was in the back with Nan and the small twins.

"All ready?" Mr. Bobbsey asked. "This is the last call. Do we have our Fat Fairy? I'm sure we'll need a fairy at Rainbow Valley."

"Here I am, Daddy," Flossie answered.

As she reached over to give her father a big hug, Freddie suddenly shouted, "Wait, Daddy! We forgot something awful important!"

"Not your shovel and sieve," Flossie said. "They're right here on the floor."

"No. Our turtle. I want Gee Gee to see the rainbow."

Bert was glad Freddie had thought of the turtle. He still wanted to know what the initials "G. G." stood for. Bert thought that the turtle probably had belonged to the woodsman, and the initials might help the Bobbseys find him.

"All right, Freddie," Mr. Bobbsey agreed. "Get Gee Gee, but hurry."

Freddie ran into the house for the turtle, which by this time was used to the twins. Freddie got into the car and held Gee Gee in a little box on his lap.

"Good-bye, everybody!" called Sam, Dinah's husband, who was going to stay home and take care of the house.

"Good-bye, Sam!" the twins shouted.

Soon they were on the road to Rainbow Valley. It was a long ride. They stopped along the way in a cool, shady grove and had a picnic of sandwiches, fruit, and chocolate milk that Dinah had prepared.

Mr. Bobbsey drove all afternoon. Finally he turned off the main highway onto a narrow country road. It led through woods filled with tall pine trees. The car was on a hill that kept going up and up. Near the top all they could see was the woods and sky.

"This must be the end of the world!" sighed Flossie, who had just awakened from a nap.

Indeed, it did seem as if the road would drop off any minute. But as they reached the crest, the road sloped down. Below them a valley stretched for miles and miles.

"This is Rainbow Valley," said Mr. Bobbsey. "You can't see the falls from here, though."

Through the center of the valley flowed a sparkling stream which became lost in the forest. Peeking through the treetops was the roof of a large building.

"That's the hotel—Rainbow House," said the twins' father.

"Where's our house?" Freddie asked. "Gee Gee wants to get out of his box and crawl around."

"The cottage is only a short walk from the hotel. We'll soon come to it."

Mr. Bobbsey went down the hill slowly. Then he drove up a long, winding driveway and stopped in front of the big white hotel. Immediately a little man in a red uniform and a flat, round red hat, tilted sideways, hurried out to meet them.

"Oh, isn't he funny?" Flossie whispered to Dinah, giggling.

"Is he a general?" Freddie asked, thinking the red suit was some sort of army uniform.

"Course not," Dinah said, laughing. "He's a porter. Some folks would call him a bellhop."

"Does he hop when he hears a bell?" Freddie asked. "I want to see him hop."

"Sh!" Dinah cautioned, because the little boy had spoken pretty loudly. "When the hotel clerk rings a bell, the bellhop jumps up to carry the guest's baggage."

Mr. Bobbsey explained to the bellhop that they were going to a cabin after a while and there was no hurry about the bags.

"Are you having supper at the hotel?" the bellhop asked.

"Yes, we are," the twins' father replied.

It was arranged that the bellhop would take Dinah to the cabin and she would show him where to put the luggage before having dinner. Meanwhile, the others walked into the hotel lobby.

It was the strangest lobby the twins had ever seen. It was filled with all sorts of stuffed animals. There were foxes, owls, squirrels, and chipmunks. A big eagle hung from the beamed ceiling by a wire.

"This looks like a museum," Bert said as he admired a stuffed fox crouching on a log.

"They all came from Rainbow Valley," spoke up a man sitting near by.

"You mean there are wild animals in these woods?" Nan asked.

"Lots of them," the man answered.

"Oh dear!" Flossie exclaimed. "I hope they won't hurt us!"

"I guess if you don't bother them, they won't bother you," the man said.

The Bobbseys went into the dining room. Although Freddie was hungry, he had a hard time keeping his mind on the food. He kept peeking out into the lobby. He finished first and wiggled on his chair.

"Please, Mother, may I be excused?" he asked.

Mrs. Bobbsey said he might, if he would promise to stay near by. But when the others finished and went out into the lobby, Freddie was not in sight.

"I think your little boy went outside," the clerk said to Mr. Bobbsey.

The family hurried out the door. Freddie was not around, and dusk was coming on. Flossie climbed into the car to see if her twin were hiding. He was not there, but the little girl made a discovery.

"Freddie's sand sieve is gone," she told her parents.

Mr. and Mrs. Bobbsey looked at each other in alarm. Had Freddie gone off by himself to look for the pot of gold at the waterfall?

# CHAPTER VI

## THE PLAYFUL RAINBOW

THE TWINS' parents held a hurried talk.
Then Mrs. Bobbsey asked Nan and Bert to take
Flossie to the cabin, while they hunted for Freddie.

Flossie burst into tears. "If Freddie's lost, I
have to find him, too!" she wailed.

"Maybe he went to the cabin," Nan suggested
hopefully.

Though Mr. and Mrs. Bobbsey were still worried, they thought the cabin a good place to
look first. Mr. Bobbsey started off almost on a
run along a path through the woods, the others
at his heels. A placard on a tree said *To Sunset
Cabin*. This was where the Bobbseys were going to stay.

They had almost reached it when they saw
a surprising sight. The short bellhop with the
red suit and tilted red cap was pushing a wheelbarrow loaded with baggage. Alongside him

marched Freddie, his own little suitcase in his hand. Perched on the side of his head was the little red sieve. He was having a hard time keeping it on. Every few seconds it would slide off and he would grab it.

"He's playing bellhop," Flossie giggled.

When Freddie heard that he had frightened his family, he said he was sorry. When he left the hotel dining room, the bellhop had just been loading the wheelbarrow with the last of the baggage from the back of the Bobbsey car. Freddie had decided to help.

Dinah came out on the porch of the one-story log cabin to greet the Bobbseys. She said the trunks had come and everything was ready. She had even unpacked pajamas and robes and the children's play clothes for the next morning.

"Then I can start digging for gold right after breakfast," Freddie announced.

"If you listen," said Dinah, "you can hear Rainbow Falls."

Everyone became silent. Yes, they could catch the distant sound. It was a little like the sound of car tires on a wet pavement, Bert declared.

"But much more beautiful than that, I'm sure," his mother smiled.

The children followed their parents into the large living room of the cabin. It had pretty blue curtains at the windows and a big fireplace at one end. Dinah showed Freddie and Bert which was the boys' bedroom, and Flossie and Nan the girls'.

Freddie and Flossie went outside again. Bert followed a few minutes later. As he reached the porch, the younger twins came racing toward him excitedly.

"We saw that man!" Flossie exclaimed.

"What man?" Bert asked.

"The man who Freddie knocked his hat off," Flossie cried out, all mixed up. She meant to say the man whose hat Freddie had knocked off.

"You mean the man at the Sportsman's Show in Lakeport?" Bert asked.

"Uh-huh," Freddie and Flossie answered together.

"Where'd he go?" Bert cried, hurrying down the steps.

"That way." Flossie pointed off among the trees.

"How long ago?"

"Just now."

Bert ran to look. He could see nobody.

"You're sure you saw him?" Bert said, running back.

Freddie and Flossie insisted that they had seen the disagreeable man. Bert might have doubted it, except that both children could not be wrong. He dashed into the cabin and told his parents and Nan about the man.

"But Mr. Smink was going to the city to keep an eye on Old Abe," Nan recalled to the others.

Everyone was puzzled. If the small twins really had seen the mysterious man, what was he doing in Rainbow Valley? Did he just happen to be near the Bobbseys' new home, or had he been spying on them, and why?

"I'm sure it has something to do with Mr. Lincoln," Nan spoke up. "Maybe he never went to the city. Maybe that man followed him here."

The twins' father said that in any case the children had better forget about him. Right now they should think about bed after their tiresome day.

When they awoke next morning, it was a warm, sunny day. Mrs. Bobbsey said Dinah might accompany the children to the falls directly after breakfast.

"I'm going to take Gee Gee," said Flossie.

She talked it over with Nan, and they decided to take along a silk thread to tie onto one of the turtle's legs. The other end would be attached to a stone Then he could swim around in the water without being lost.

When Dinah was ready, Flossie got the turtle and Freddie took his shovel and sieve. The twins skipped down the path ahead of Dinah on their way to the falls. The noise of the water grew louder as they came closer to it.

"There it is!" Bert shouted.

Ahead of them was a steep cliff, which had a right-angle turn at the end of it. Down over the corner rushed a swift current of water. It tumbled and foamed into the river below, sending up a cloud of spray.

"I see the rainbow!" Flossie exclaimed.

"How beautiful!" Nan cried.

"It's all the colors of ice cream," Freddie shouted. "Pink and orange and yellow and . . ." Freddie was all out of breath and could not finish. Indeed, the falls were a wonderful sight. The sun, shining through the mist, made a beautiful, arched rainbow.

"Gracious sakes," Dinah said, "this rainbow lasts all day long. You children will have plenty of time to find the pot o' gold!"

"Where should we look, Dinah?" Freddie asked.

"At the end of the rainbow, I guess."

"But it has two ends," he said.

"You'd better stay on this side of the river," Dinah said, looking across the swift stream to the slippery rock cliff that rose straight up.

"I'd like to try climbing up there sometime," said Bert.

"You'd better not," Dinah advised, "unless you could turn yourself into a spider."

The twins laughed. Freddie and Flossie ran over to a spot that seemed to be the end of the rainbow. But when they got there, the end of the rainbow appeared to be at another place.

"I wish this rainbow would stand still," Freddie said. "But I'll dig here, anyway."

He pushed his shovel down into the stony bank of the stream. Flossie went back to set Gee Gee free. Dinah helped tie the silk cord to one of his legs, and made a loop at the other end for Flossie to put over a stone. Gee Gee seemed very happy with this arrangement, and paddled out onto the water.

Dinah sat down under a big pine tree to watch the children play. "How you getting on with the pot o' gold?" she called to Freddie.

Freddie was dumping some wet gravel into his sieve. "I've only got yellow pebbles," he answered. "But I'll find some gold!"

The older twins, meanwhile, were throwing sticks into the water. They were carried downstream like little boats. Suddenly Bert shouted, "Look! What's that thing that just came over the falls?"

Something was bobbing up and down in the bubbling water. Bert grabbed a long stick and reached far out into the stream. He managed to snag the object.

"It's a basket," the boy said, as he drew it to the shore.

Nan picked it up. "Bert," she exclaimed excitedly, "it's just like the baskets Mr. Lincoln was selling at the Sportsman's Show!"

"You're right," Bert agreed. He turned the basket over and over in his hands.

The twins gazed at the top of the waterfall. Had the basket been tossed away by someone to whom the old woodsman had sold it? Or had he himself dropped it somewhere up in that mysterious forest above Rainbow Falls?

As the Bobbseys stood silent, trying to find an answer to their questions, Dinah gave a sudden shriek. Standing among the trees near Bert and Nan was a big black bear! It sniffed the air a moment. Then the bear dropped down on all fours and came directly toward the twins!

# CHAPTER VII

NAN'S STRANGE PET

"RUN!" Dinah shouted, as the bear came toward Nan and Bert.

She grabbed Freddie and Flossie by the hand and started to hurry off. Bert picked up a stick. He would hit the bear on the nose if he came too close!

"Run!" Dinah called again.

But Nan had another idea. She remembered that the guest at the hotel had said the wild animals in Rainbow Valley probably would not harm the children if they did not harm the animals. It seemed to Nan as if the oncoming bear had a friendly look in its eyes.

"Maybe it's tame," she said to Bert, who was holding the stick ready.

Then Nan noticed that the bear was wearing a collar from which dangled a broken chain. A wild thought occurred to her. Could this be Mr. Lincoln's tame bear?

"Run!" screamed Dinah. The big black bear was only ten feet from the older twins.

"Up, Kate!" Nan cried suddenly. This was what the old woodsman had told the twins he said to his pet bear.

The big animal stopped in its tracks. Again Nan called, "Up, Kate!"

This time the bear bent its head slowly to the ground. Then, raising its hind feet in the air, the bear stood on its head!

"It is Kate! It is Kate!" Nan shouted gleefully.

The bear rolled over and then walked up to the twins. She sat on her haunches, and Nan stroked her head. Bert put down the stick and patted the animal. So did Freddie and Flossie and Dinah, when they were sure it was safe.

"Kate's *beeyootiful!*" exclaimed Flossie. "I want to take her home."

"Now that's goin' a little too far," Dinah declared. "You play with her here."

Freddie thought he would like to make the bear stand on her head.

"Up, Kate!" he cried. But the bear did not move.

Bert tried. The bear paid no attention. Flossie took a turn. But the bear just looked at her.

"You try it, Dinah," Bert said, laughing.

Dinah was over her fright now. She chuckled and said, "Up, Kate!" But the bear looked off among the trees.

Presently Nan tried again. At once Kate stood on her head.

"She's your pet!" Bert cried. "Kate won't do tricks for anybody but you."

Nan felt rather proud that the bear would obey her. She gave Kate a little hug.

Presently Dinah said it was time to go back to the cabin. To the twins' surprise and delight, Kate followed Nan.

"I guess you sure enough found yourself a playmate," said Dinah.

Mr. and Mrs. Bobbsey were amazed to see their twins arriving with a tame bear. Nan used the broken chain to tie Kate to a tree in back of the cabin. Soon several neighbors heard about the bear and came to look at her. Nan made Kate stand on her head. The bear never seemed to get tired of doing the trick.

Bert asked the people if they knew Mr. Lincoln, the woodsman. Nobody had heard of him, nor of anyone called Old Abe, nor of a Mr. Smink.

"If Kate ran away from Mr. Lincoln," Bert told his parents, "Mr. Lincoln surely must be in these woods somewhere."

"Not necessarily," said Mrs. Bobbsey. "He may have left Kate with a friend and she broke away."

Bert was not convinced. He showed them the basket which had come over the waterfall.

"Even if Mr. Lincoln went to the city, maybe he came back," the boy argued.

"Well, suppose you inquire about him at the hotel," his father suggested.

During luncheon Flossie said that they ought to make a bed for Kate. Her mother smiled, saying, "Bears just sleep on the ground wherever they happen to be."

"But Mother," Flossie insisted, "if Kate sleeps on the ground and catches a cold in her head, she won't be able to stand on it!"

Everyone laughed, and Freddie said, "Let's make her a bed of straw like horses have."

He knew that the hotel had riding horses and asked Bert to take them to the stables to get some straw. Bert agreed and took the little twins to the stables before inquiring about Mr. Lincoln.

When they got to the stables, they saw several horses looking over the half-doors of their stalls and swishing their tails to keep the flies off. A man sitting on a box in front of the stables looked up and said, "You children want to ride?"

"We don't want to ride," Flossie answered "We want a bed for our bear."

The man was so startled that he almost fell off the box. "A bear!" he exclaimed. "What will these vacation people bring here next?"

"We didn't bring her," Freddie said. "We found her here."

The man gave Bert a queer look as if he did not believe the story.

"That's right," Bert said. "We found a tame bear and would like some straw for her to sleep on."

The man laughed and pointed to a pile of clean straw. "Help yourself," he said.

The three children gathered armfuls of straw and hurried back to Kate. Bert left the younger twins to make a bed for the bear, and returned to the hotel. A man he had not seen before was on duty at the desk. When Bert asked him about the old woodsman, the clerk said he had never heard of him.

"We have a guest here named Lincoln," the man said. "He may be a relative. Why don't you ask him? He's in room thirty-two."

Hopefully Bert went there and knocked on the door. It was opened by a fat man with a jolly face.

"Are you Mr. Lincoln?" Bert asked.

"Yes," he replied. "Did you hope to find a tall man with a beard?" he asked, laughing.

"Why—uh—yes," Bert replied, astonished. "Have you a brother or a cousin who's a woodsman around here?"

"No, but I'd like to know who this Mr. Lincoln is," the man said. "You're the second person in two days to ask me about him."

Bert at once thought of the unpleasant man whom Flossie and Freddie insisted they had seen. The boy described Mr. Smink and asked if he were the man who had inquired.

"That's the man. He said his name was Calter," the fat man told Bert.

"Is he staying at the hotel?" the boy asked excitedly.

"I don't know, but Possum might."

"Possum?" Bert repeated.

"The little bellhop who wears the red suit. I don't know how he got his name."

Bert went off to find the bellhop, and asked him how he had received the nickname. The little man told Bert that he had worked at the hotel ever since it was built.

"In the early days," he said, "I worked all evening. Sometimes I would take a nap sitting on a chair in the lobby. But I was always sure to keep one eye open. When anybody called 'boy' I would hop right up. People said I was just pretending to be asleep, the way an opossum does. That's how I got the name of Possum. Now what can I do for you?" he asked.

"Is a man named Calter staying here?"

"No."

"Do you know a woodsman around here named Mr. Lincoln? He might be called Old Abe."

Possum thought for a moment. "No, I don't know any woodsman by that name," he said.

Bert told the bellhop about the mysterious Mr. Lincoln, the knife he had lost, Kate, the bear they thought was his, and finally about the basket which had come over the waterfall.

"We've seen those baskets!" Possum exclaimed. "A ghost leaves them."

# CHAPTER VIII

## THE SINGING WATERFALL

A GHOST! Bert could hardly believe his ears. Possum told him about a mysterious person who had been leaving beautifully woven baskets at the cottagers' doors during the night. Inside were notes asking for food in return for his gifts.

"This week he's been asking for milk," Possum said. "Just why, nobody seems to know."

"Do the people leave food?" Bert asked.

"They sure do," the bellhop replied. "He goes to a different cabin every night. Next morning the food's gone. But nobody ever sees the ghost."

Bert asked if Possum knew where the ghost was supposed to come that night.

"I think to Mrs. Bennington's. Her cabin's not far from yours."

Bert raced all the way home and asked permission to sleep outdoors that night and try to trap the ghost.

"I could use Dad's sleeping bag," said Bert,

54

"and stay close to Mrs. Bennington's porch."

At first Mrs. Bobbsey was unwilling, but finally she agreed to let Bert try to catch the ghost if Mrs. Bennington would permit it.

"Oh, yes," said Mrs. Bennington, when they spoke to her, "the ghost left us a basket last night and we're to leave him food this evening."

Bert asked if she would show him the basket. Mrs. Bennington got it. The unusual basket was just like the one Bert had found in the stream.

For once Bert could hardly wait for night to come.

Flossie, meanwhile, ran to her bedroom window, which looked out on the back yard of the cabin, where Kate was.

"I think she's going to use her straw bed," she said.

The other twins came running to Flossie's side, followed by Mrs. Bobbsey and Dinah. They all watched the bear. She walked around and around. Finally she lay down on the straw Freddie and Flossie had prepared.

"Oh goody!" the small twins cried out.

Mrs. Bobbsey had to admit she was surprised. She had not thought Kate would bother with the bed.

"I'm going now, Mother," Bert announced half an hour later. He kissed her good night and started for Mrs. Bennington's with the sleeping bag. A few minutes later, as he was crawling into it, Mrs. Bennington put a large bag of food and a bottle of milk on the porch steps near by. She waved to Bert and wished him luck.

Soon it became very dark. The only sounds were the chirping of tree toads and the distant thunder of the falls.

An hour passed and Bert became very sleepy. Suddenly he awoke with a start. He had been asleep! Bert got out of the sleeping bag and went to the porch. The food was still there. The ghost had not come yet.

But what had awakened Bert? He listened as he got back into the sleeping bag. All at once an owl hooted in the tree above him. That must have been what had awakened him. He kept his eye on the porch, listening and listening for the ghost . . .

The sun was shining above the rim of the forest when Bert awoke. Birds were singing and the falls sounded very far away.

Bert glanced at the porch. The bag of food and the bottle of milk were still there. The ghost had not come!

Disappointed, Bert went back to Sunset Cabin. Only Dinah was up.

"Did you catch the ghost?" she asked.

Bert told the story. "Dinah, I think the ghost is Mr. Lincoln. Maybe he's in trouble and that's why he didn't come."

In a little while the rest of the family got up. When they heard the story, Nan became as concerned as Bert about Mr. Lincoln. Their parents begged the twins to put the mystery out of their minds for a while and have some fun.

"I'll take you to town later to make inquiries," Mr. Bobbsey promised Bert.

"I want you to meet some of the other boys and girls here at Rainbow House," said Mrs. Bobbsey, "and there are all sorts of games on the playground next to the hotel."

The twins skipped off to various places. Nan went to feed Kate. Soon a crowd of boys and girls who wanted to watch the bear and see her stand on her head, gathered in back of the Bobbsey cabin. Almost overnight Nan had become the most popular girl at Rainbow House!

All the Bobbsey children had a wonderful time that day. Directly after supper Flossie came running to her mother.

"Dinah didn't play all day, Mommy," she said seriously, "and Gee Gee hasn't had a swim, and my 'chanical fish didn't even get wet!"

Mrs. Bobbsey smiled. "And you want to do something about it?"

Flossie said she thought she should take them down to Rainbow Falls. Mrs. Bobbsey agreed, so Dinah and Freddie and Flossie and Gee Gee and the mechanical fish set out. No one else was at the falls. The silk cord was tied to Gee Gee, and he swam around in the water happily.

Freddie found a little sandy pool near the edge of the swirling stream. "Here's a good place for our fish to swim," he cried. Dinah thought so, too. She wound up the fish for the twins and they put them in the water. The fish wiggled this way and that.

"Now I'll catch mine," Freddie said, holding out his special pole from the Sportsman's Show.

While he was trying to make the magnetic bait touch the mechanical fish's nose, Flossie looked at Dinah.

"That's an awful pretty song you're humming," she said.

Dinah looked surprised. "I'm not humming," she said.

"Well, who is, then?" the little girl asked. "Don't you hear it, Freddie?"

The three stood still and listened. Above the roar of the waterfall came a beautiful singing sound. It grew louder, until the air was filled with the music of a lovely soprano voice.

Dinah and the children looked in every direction. Not a person was in sight. All at once the singing stopped.

"It's magic!" Flossie exclaimed. "This is the magic Rainbow Falls. A fairy lives here!"

"That sure sounded like a lovely fairy's song," Dinah agreed.

The twins were eager to run home and tell the others about the fairy in the waterfall. They ran up the cool, pine-needle path back to their cabin, with Dinah after them.

"Mother," Flossie cried, "there's a fairy in the falls who has the most *beeyootiful* voice!"

Mrs. Bobbsey looked at her daughter, amused. What an imagination her little girl had!

"That's right, Mrs. Bobbsey," Dinah spoke up. "Somebody *was* singing down near the waterfall."

Dinah was telling about the lovely voice when Bert and Nan ran up. At once they wanted to go down and hear it themselves.

Flossie offered to put Gee Gee and the fish away, and pick up all the toys, while Nan and Bert went down to the falls with Freddie. Dusk was settling over the woodland when the three children arrived at the spot. The rainbow had gone, because the sun had set.

"Here's where the fairy lives," Freddie said importantly.

The older twins listened. There was no humming or singing.

"Gosh," Freddie said in disappointment.

"Come on," Bert said. "We'd better get home while we can still see the path."

They had walked only a few steps from the shore when the strange humming suddenly filled the air again. Then a clear, bell-like voice began to sing a beautiful tune without words.

"There's the fairy!" Freddie whispered. "Didn't I tell you?"

Bert and Nan looked at each other startled. The voice certainly did seem to come right out of the foaming water!

"*Who* can it *be?*" Nan said, when the singing stopped a few moments later.

The older twins were so astonished that they did not notice Freddie. He was doing a little investigating of his own. Now he was very close to the falls, and was stepping from stone to stone out into the stream.

Suddenly Bert saw him. "Freddie, come back!" he cried out.

But Bert spoke too late. At that moment Freddie slipped. The next second he plunged into the churning water and disappeared!

# CHAPTER IX

"FREDDIE!" Nan screamed.

She put her hands over her eyes to shut out the awful sight of her little brother disappearing under the falls.

Bert stood absolutely still for an instant, holding his breath. Then he started to run along the edge of the stream. He was sure the water which had carried Freddie down would also carry the small boy along. In a moment he should come to the surface.

"I'll get him," Bert shouted to his sister encouragingly.

In the dusk it was hard to see very well. There were deep shadows on the swirling water. Twice Bert thought he saw Freddie, but the black masses were only leaves floating in Rainbow River.

"I see him!" Nan called.

She had run after Bert. Now she pointed to the middle of the stream. A head bobbed above the water.

"I'll get him!" Bert said.

He kicked off his moccasins and waded in. Starting to swim, he went toward what he thought was his small brother.

Nan, waiting on shore, suddenly realized that the head was much larger than Freddie's. Then she could see whiskers. That wasn't Freddie!

Once more Nan became fearful about her little brother. Just as she was going to call out to Bert, she saw that the man in the water was holding Freddie in one arm.

To her amazement the man swam farther downstream. With a few more swift strokes, he reached the bank and laid Freddie down. Bert had tried to reach them, but the man had outdistanced him. As Nan ran toward them, the stranger suddenly dived back into the water and swam away rapidly.

"Freddie! Freddie!" Nan cried, rushing up to her small brother and dropping to her knees. "Are you all right?"

She turned him over on his stomach, and began to give him artificial respiration, as she had learned to do at school.

"L-l-leave me alone," Freddie begged weakly.

Nan sighed in relief. She turned Freddie on his back, and told him to lie still and rest.

By the time Bert came up, Freddie was ready to talk. He said that when the water had carried him down and down, he had held his breath. Then, just when the little boy thought he could not hold it any longer, someone had grabbed him and brought him to the top of the water. Freddie looked all around.

"Where is he?" the little boy asked.

Nan said the man had swum off before they could find out who he was.

"He evidently didn't want us to see him," said Bert. "Do you suppose he was Mr. Lincoln?"

"When you find him, Bert," said Freddie, "I want to thank him."

Nan thought they had better go back to the cabin at once. Freddie was soaking wet and the evening was cool.

The little boy was sorry he had not found out where the fairy singing came from. He begged to stay a little longer. But he was beginning to shiver and Nan insisted that they leave.

When Mr. and Mrs. Bobbsey and Dinah heard about Freddie's adventure, they were shocked.

They warned all the children to be extremely careful when playing near the water.

"This place is haunted," Dinah insisted. "Ghosts, and fairy music coming out of the water, and—" She hustled Freddie off to the boys' bedroom to get him out of his wet clothes.

All the twins except Freddie went out to say good night to Kate before going to bed. They found the old bear scratching her back against the trunk of a tree. But she flopped down eagerly as she got a whiff of the pot of honey Nan was holding behind her back.

"We'll play with you in the morning," said Flossie, "if the ghost doesn't come in the night and take you away."

But in the morning old Kate was still there. They gave her some breakfast of cereal and milk with a sugar bun. Then Freddie announced that he wanted to continue his hunt for the pot of gold. Mrs. Bobbsey said he should play near the cabin and pretend there was a rainbow there.

"I'll be the gold miner," said the little boy to his twin. "Flossie, you can be my wife. You'll stay home with all the children while I go digging."

"Be very careful, my good husband," Flossie said—she had once read this phrase in a fairy tale.

She ran to get two of the dolls she had brought along, and set up housekeeping not far from the bear. There was a large pit of sand near by, where the older children, and the mothers and fathers sometimes played horseshoes. Flossie decided to put her "children" out in this sunny place to play.

Meanwhile, Freddie put on his oldest clothes, borrowed his father's cap, and pulled it down to look like a miner's. Then he got his sand shovel and began to dig.

Bert already had started for town with his father to see if they could find anyone who knew Mr. Lincoln, the woodsman. The boy was determined to find out if the old man was in the vicinity, and return his knife to him.

They had been gone only a few minutes when Nan, who was helping her mother in the house, heard Flossie shriek. They rushed outside.

The little girl was digging furiously in the horseshoe pit. She was lying flat on her stomach and scooping out handfuls of sand as fast as she could.

"What's the matter, Flossie?" her mother asked.

"I think the pot of gold is under here," Flossie replied.

The little girl said she had pushed a stick

down through the sand and hit something hard. Freddie came running over. He was disappointed that his twin might be about to uncover the pot of gold he wanted to find.

"Somebody help me," said Flossie.

Freddie rushed back to his own digging place and brought the shovel. Nan quickly made a hole in the sand with it. The shovel hit something hard.

"It's mine! Let me pick it up," Flossie said.

Nan stepped back and let her small sister tug at the treasure. Finally she pulled up a large, rusty coffee can.

"The treasure's inside!" Flossie said excitedly.

She pulled at the lid, but it would not come off.

"Let me try it," said Mrs. Bobbsey.

She could not budge the lid either, so she took the shovel and hammered it against the metal edge. Finally the lid fell off.

The children and their mother peeked inside.

"Huh!" said Freddie. "It's only a lot of old papers." He was secretly glad his twin had not found the treasure ahead of him.

Reaching her hand inside the can, Mrs. Bobbsey pulled out the sheets of paper, which had been torn from a magazine. The top sheet was entitled *Indian Trails of Rainbow Mountain.*

"Rainbow Mountain?" Nan repeated. "Why, this is Rainbow Mountain."

"I guess the person who tore out the pages was ashamed of himself," Flossie said, "so he hid them in the can and buried it."

Mrs. Bobbsey said it was a mystery indeed. She could not see, however, why anyone should bother to hide the papers. As she looked at them more closely, the twins' mother found "Rainbow House Library" stamped on the first one.

"Somebody took them from the hotel library!" she exclaimed.

While the Bobbseys were discussing the strange incident, a group of children came running up. They had heard the talking, and wondered what was going on. When a boy named Johnny Wyman heard the story, he began to laugh.

"I put those papers in there just yesterday," he said. "I'm going to have a party, and that was going to be part of the treasure hunt."

Mrs. Bobbsey looked at him reprovingly. She asked him why he had not returned the article to the library instead of burying it.

Johnny was surprised. He said he had found the pages in the woods and thought that they had been thrown away. He had not noticed that they belonged to the hotel library.

Nan suddenly had a hunch. The torn pages from the magazine might have something to do with the mystery of Mr. Lincoln.

"Mother," she said, "please let me return them to the hotel library."

"All right, dear," said Mrs. Bobbsey. "Suppose you go right now."

The small twins continued their hunt for the pot of gold, and Mrs. Bobbsey returned to the cabin. Nan hurried off to the hotel and went straight to the library.

At a desk sat a pretty, middle-aged woman. A little sign in front of her said *Miss Taylor*. She smiled up at Nan.

"Can I help you find a book?" she asked. "What would you like?"

Nan laid the torn pages on the desk and explained how Flossie had found them. Miss Taylor looked at the pages. Then she said excitedly, "That dreadful man! I should get the police after him!"

# CHAPTER X

## THE MYSTERY MAN

NAN BOBBSEY looked at the librarian in amazement. Finally she asked what man Miss Taylor meant.

"I don't think he used his right name," the librarian answered. "He said it was Calter."

That was the name the hotel guest had mentioned to Bert, Nan recalled.

Miss Taylor went on to explain that a very unpleasant, middle-aged man had come into the library several times. He had pulled books from the cases and not put them back. He had even torn a page from one and made notes on it.

"When I spoke to him about this," Miss Taylor added, "Mr. Calter said he was a guest of the hotel and had a right to do as he pleased. He seemed particularly interested in this article you've just brought back."

Miss Taylor said that she had found out that the man was not a guest at the hotel at all.

"He must have wanted this torn-out part pretty badly," Nan said. "What is it about?"

Miss Taylor glanced through it. Presently she said, "Part of it's about old secret trails."

"In these mountains?" Nan asked her.

"Yes," she replied. "It seems to me—" She paused. "Yes, here it is." She read a sentence. " 'It is thought that one of the secret trails was somewhere back of Rainbow Falls.' "

Nan asked what Mr. Calter looked like.

"He was tall and thin, and had black eyes."

Nan was sure he was the man they knew as Mr. Smink.

"If Mr. Calter ever comes back," Nan said to Miss Taylor, "please try to find out more about him."

"Indeed I will," the librarian promised.

On the way back to the cabin, Nan spied some unusual-looking flowers a little distance off the path.

"Mother would love these," she told herself. "I think I'll pick some."

Nan broke off several of the tall, light blue flowers, which she thought were foxgloves. Then a little farther among the trees she noticed some dainty lady-slippers. After picking several, she looked ahead of her in the woods. What were those beautiful, deep pink flowers near the base of that big tree?

Without realizing it, Nan was walking deeper and deeper into the woods. She was about to pick some of the pink flowers, when she tripped on a tree root and sat down suddenly.

She did not get up at once. It was so beautiful all around her that she just sat still to take it all in. Suddenly the quiet was broken.

"Someone's coming," Nan thought. "Maybe another girl looking for flowers."

She got up and looked. It was not a girl but a man going through the woods. His back was turned to her. He seemed to be looking for something on the ground. Suddenly he turned and saw Nan Bobbsey. His small eyes grew even more narrow. Then he started to run back the way he had come.

"It's Mr. Smink!" Nan gasped.

The man did not stop and in a few moments disappeared. Nan found her way home. After telling her mother about seeing Mr. Smink, she said, "What do you suppose he was looking for?"

"I don't know, Nan," her mother said, "but you shouldn't go so far into the woods by yourself. You might have gotten lost. Promise me you won't go in there alone again."

Nan was sorry she had worried her mother and promised. Then she went back to the hotel and told Miss Taylor about seeing Smink-Calter.

"Mother won't let me go out in the woods alone any more," Nan told the librarian. "Would you go with me and see if we can find him?"

The librarian said she would be very glad to go. The library would close in a few minutes. Miss Taylor said that after Nan had left, she had discovered a pamphlet missing from the shelves.

"I suspect that awful man took it when he took the magazine article," she said.

"What was it about?" Nan asked.

"It was a legend about Rainbow Falls," Miss Taylor replied. "I had planned to read it but hadn't had time yet. It was called *The Feathered Rainbow.*"

Nan was sorry she had not read the pamphlet. It was just possible something in it might have helped solve the mystery of Rainbow Falls.

Ten minutes later she and Miss Taylor started out together. Nan led the way to the spot where she had seen Mr. Smink. They found his footprints easily, and tried to figure out what he had been looking for.

"There's nothing here," Miss Taylor said

finally. "Perhaps we had better start back now."

Nan begged that they search a little farther.

They pushed on. For a time they had been so far away from the falls that they had not heard the noise of the thundering water. Now they could hear it clearly. They also heard something else. Someone was chopping wood.

"Maybe it's the woodsman!" Nan exclaimed.

Quickly she told the librarian about Mr. Lincoln, and they went toward the sound. It stopped suddenly, and they were not sure which way to go. They searched all around but could find no one.

"Listen!" Nan whispered.

She was sure she had heard the beautiful, mysterious singing. Miss Taylor heard it, too. The singing did not last long at a time. It sounded as if someone were practicing part of a song over and over.

"I'm sure the singer isn't far away," Nan said excitedly. "Come on!"

She and Miss Taylor scrambled among the bushes and briers. Presently they noticed a man standing a little distance ahead, his back to them. Evidently he was listening to the singing.

Nan and the librarian moved closer. All at once Miss Taylor said to Nan in a whisper:

"That's Mr. Calter!"

"We'd better not make any noise," Nan advised, recognizing him as Mr. Smink, "or he'll run away again."

She and Miss Taylor went ahead on tiptoe. The man paid no attention, until they were right in back of him. Then suddenly he turned around. For a moment Mr. Smink looked as if he were seeing ghosts. Then he said harshly, "What do you want?"

"We want to ask you a few questions," the librarian answered. "You took the article *Indian Trails of Rainbow Mountain,* didn't you?"

"I did not!"

"You said you were staying at the hotel, but you weren't," Miss Taylor reminded him.

The man glared at her and Nan Bobbsey. "Get out of here!" he ordered roughly.

Nan felt a little frightened, but Miss Taylor did not pay any attention to his command.

"You'll tell me what you did with that pamphlet called *The Feathered Rainbow* before I move a step," she answered.

"Is that so?" Mr. Smink snarled.

With that he came toward them. Nan, frightened, stepped back. Suddenly Miss Taylor grabbed the girl's arm.

"Look out!" she cried. "The ravine! It's right behind you!"

Nan tried to stop, but it was too late. The earth gave way at the edge of the embankment. Nan and Miss Taylor both lost their balance and down they went over the side of the steep ravine.

# CHAPTER XI

NAN STARTED to roll downhill. At the foot of the ravine was a small, rocky stream which ran into Rainbow River.

"I mustn't let myself roll down!" Nan told herself wildly.

She reached out an arm and grabbed hold of a small tree trunk. It took all her strength to hold on. But she was safe!

Nan looked around, wondering what had happened to Miss Taylor. Her friend lay a short distance away, her eyes closed.

"Oh, she must be hurt!" Nan thought.

Inch by inch the little girl crawled across the steep embankment. She grasped at bushes and rocks to keep from losing her balance. At last Nan reached Miss Taylor. In a few seconds the librarian opened her eyes. She put her hand to her head.

"Are you all right?" Nan asked her.

"My head hurts dreadfully. I hit it on a stone. Are you all right, Nan?"

The twin said that she was. Miss Taylor felt a little dizzy, but with Nan's help she managed to get to the top of the embankment. She said she would rest a few minutes, then they would go on. Miss Taylor was more angry than ever at Mr. Smink.

"He certainly didn't care whether we were hurt or not," she said. "I wonder where he went."

Nan would have liked to find out, but Miss Taylor was too upset to do this now. And Nan had promised her mother not to go off in the woods alone.

"We'd better go home," the librarian said, getting up. They walked back slowly to the hotel. Then Nan hurried on to the Bobbsey cabin.

No one was there but Dinah. The cook said Mrs. Bobbsey had gone off with the small twins in a great hurry. It had something to do with the bear.

"Oh, is Kate gone?" Nan asked.

"No," Dinah answered. "But I believe she's going to go."

Nan was sorry to hear this and ran outside to where the bear was tied. Kate seemed to want to play, so Nan unfastened the chain. Then she said, "Up, Kate!"

The bear obeyed her. While Kate was standing on her head, a voice behind Nan exclaimed, "How wonderful!"

A young woman came up. Smiling at Nan, she explained that she was the children's hostess at the hotel. She was planning a hobby show for them.

"Wouldn't you like to put the bear in the show?" she asked Nan.

"I'd love to," Nan replied, "but this bear doesn't belong to me, and his master may come to get him any time."

The hostess, whose name was Mrs. Nixon, was disappointed. She asked Nan to try to keep the bear until after the show.

Nan thought it would be exciting to make Kate do her tricks in the show. She promised to see if she could keep the old bear a few days longer. After Mrs. Nixon had left, Nan began to wonder how she might keep Kate's owner from taking her.

"Maybe Mother can help me," the girl thought.

She waited for her mother and the small twins to return. An hour went by, but they did not come back. Nan had promised to go to the hotel and have luncheon with a girl named Sarah Willets, whom she had met the day before.

She decided to write a note asking that no one take the bear away before she returned. Then she tied the note to Kate's collar.

As she walked to the hotel, Nan wondered where her mother and the small twins had gone. And had Bert and Mr. Bobbsey found out anything in town about Mr. Lincoln?

At this very moment, Bert was busy asking storekeepers in Westbrook if they knew Mr. Lincoln. He had already been to a butcher shop. The butcher had said, sure, he knew a Mr. Lincoln. But the man was only about twenty-five years old instead of sixty.

Next Bert had gone to Sayre's Drugstore. He had not found out anything there about Mr. Lincoln. But he had learned that Sayre's sold the biggest double-dip ice cream cone he had ever seen!

"I'll come back later and get one," Bert promised, grinning, as he went on to a stationery and newspaper store. Maybe the woodsman bought a newspaper once in a while. But the stationer had never heard of an old woodsman with whiskers, named Lincoln.

Bert was growing discouraged. He had promised to meet his father in an hour. Half an hour had gone by already.

"What'll I try next?" he wondered. "Let's

see, Mr. Lincoln must have to have his shoes mended. I'll go to the shoemaker."

He found a shoe-repairing shop and asked the stout, jolly proprietor what he wanted to know.

"No, I have never heard of a Mr. Lincoln," said the shoemaker. "What's he look like?"

Bert told him about the tall man with whiskers and said he owned a bear named Kate. Right now the Bobbseys had the bear, and wanted to let Mr. Lincoln know.

"Why don't you let the bear loose?" the shoemaker suggested. "He probably would find his way back alone to his master."

Bert admitted he had never thought of this. Secretly he hoped they might keep the bear all summer.

Bert had been so busy talking to the shoemaker that he had not noticed a boy standing in the doorway. Now the boy walked in and said, "Hiya, Bert."

It was Danny Rugg!

"So you have a bear, eh?" said Danny. "Where is he? I want to see him."

Bert told the boy from Lakeport that they were staying at Rainbow House, but he did not invite Danny to visit him. He had not forgotten how Danny had nearly ruined the motorboat at the Sportsman's Show.

"Where are you staying?" he asked Danny.

The boy said he and his mother and father were at Red Ridge Lodge, and that it was a much better place than Rainbow House. Bert ignored this rude statement.

Danny wanted to know who Mr. Lincoln was. So the boy had heard the whole conversation! Bert told him he was the old woodsman who had sold baskets at the Sportsman's Show. Danny was interested at once.

"You think he lives around here?" he asked.

"Maybe," said Bert shortly, and walked out of the shoemaker's shop. He hurried up the street, hoping Danny would not follow. Quickly he went around a corner and down a side street. He looked back. Danny was not in sight.

Bert hurried into a hardware store, which had a display of rifles in the window. Maybe Mr. Lincoln had purchased one at this store. The boy found a clerk and asked if he knew a woodsman named Mr. Lincoln. The man started to shake his head, then said, "Wait a minute now. There was an old fellow in here—what was his name?"

While the man was trying to recall it, into the store burst Danny Rugg. Bert was disgusted. He was not going to have Danny find out any more!

"I'll get rid of him," Bert thought quickly.

Going up to Danny, he asked him how he would like to have the biggest double-dip ice cream cone he had ever seen. Bert said he would even pay for it, and grinned.

"Get me one, too," he ordered, pushing a fifty-cent piece into Danny's hand. "You get the cones up at Sayre's. I'll meet you there."

Danny turned on his heel and ran from the store. Bert walked back to the clerk.

"Have you thought of the name?" he asked.

"No," the man answered. "The fact is, I don't think I ever heard his last name."

Bert was disappointed. He thanked the clerk and was about to leave, when the man added, "But I remember somebody called him Old Abe."

Bert Bobbsey leaned over the counter excitedly. He was sure he was on Mr. Lincoln's trail at last!

# CHAPTER XII

## THE BALLOON MAN

"WHERE is he? How can I find him?" Bert asked excitedly.

The hardware man shrugged. "Why are you so interested in Old Abe?" he asked.

"I think Old Abe may be the owner of a bear we have," the boy answered. "Do you know where he lives?"

The hardware man said he had no idea. A person could live comfortably almost any place on the mountain.

"Do you know if anyone lives above the falls?" Bert asked.

"I doubt it," the man answered. "Anybody who values his life won't try to go up there."

The clerk added that there were loose rocks on the cliff. Crawling straight up would be almost impossible for a human being.

"I reckon maybe Indians tried it," said the man. "But white men aren't so sure-footed as Indians."

Just then a customer came into the store. The clerk went over to wait on him.

"Well, son, let me know if you find out anything about Old Abe," he called as Bert left the store.

"I will," Bert promised. "And thanks a lot."

He went to Sayre's Drugstore where Danny Rugg was waiting with the two double-dip ice cream cones. He was already halfway through his. He asked Bert question after question, trying to find out more about Mr. Lincoln and the black bear. But Bert gave him very little information.

Mr. Bobbsey came along the street a few moments later. He was surprised to see Danny Rugg, and said he hoped the boy and his parents would have a nice vacation. He told Bert that they must go back to the cabin now.

"That is, after you get me one of those one-man meals, Bert," Mr. Bobbsey grinned.

Bert bought another cone. Then the two Bobbseys went up the street, joking about their whopping refreshment. Bert's father said they had better eat them before getting into the car, or Mrs. Bobbsey would surely scold them for spotting the cushions with the drippy ice cream.

Upon reaching the cabin half an hour later, they were surprised to find Dinah there alone.

She was fussing because she had a fine luncheon prepared and no one had come to eat it.

Mrs. Bobbsey had not planned to stay away so long with the small twins, but she had found it impossible to get back. Freddie had heard someone say there was a small zoo in the town of Red Ridge, on the other side of the mountain.

Freddie also had heard that a bear was missing from the zoo. Maybe it was Kate! Mrs. Bobbsey had consented to go, and they had made the bus just in time.

Right now they were talking to the owner of the zoo. He said the story about a bear escaping from his place was not true. In fact, he had no bears.

"We do," Flossie spoke up.

"Is he a runaway bear?" the zoo keeper asked her, smiling.

"No," Flossie replied, "he's a broken-away bear."

The man laughed and asked what she meant. Freddie knew. He explained that when his sister Nan had found the bear, Kate had had only part of her chain on.

"She broke away from the rest of the chain," Flossie added.

Mrs. Bobbsey said the bear was no trouble, but she thought perhaps Kate was not too happy living near the cabin. She had no other animals to play with. Perhaps she would be more content at the zoo.

"Oh, please, don't give her away," Flossie pleaded.

The zoo keeper said he had no room for a bear anyway, and Flossie was happy again. Freddie had walked off to look at the other animals and birds. He especially liked the giraffe, who had no top to his cage.

"His neck is so long, I guess they don't have enough wire," he told his twin, as she ran to his side.

The little girl giggled. Then she pointed out a large pool of water. Seals were playing in it. What fun they were having!

They seemed to be playing a game of tag. Just as one seal got ready to tag the tail of another, down would go the first one under the water. The second seal then would dive. Up would come the first one. This went on and on.

"Seals can do tricks," Flossie spoke up. "Why don't we make them hold something on their noses?"

Freddie thought this was a good idea. He looked around for something to toss to the seals. Then he saw a man holding a lot of balloons.

"Come on, Floss," he cried, pointing to the man.

The twins ran to him. "I want a balloon for the seal to hold on his nose," Freddie announced. "How much is it?"

The balloon man had a boy and girl of his own and liked to tease children. He said, "Ten cents for the seal, and nothing for you."

"What do you mean?" Freddie asked him.

The balloon man said it was easy for a seal to bounce a balloon up and down on his nose. For that it would cost Freddie ten cents, which was the regular price.

"But if *you* can bounce a balloon on *your* nose," the man said to Freddie, "I'll give it to you for nothing."

Flossie clapped her hands. She begged to try it as well as Freddie. The little girl picked out a blue balloon just the color of her eyes. Freddie chose a yellow one.

The man let the gas out of them so they would not blow away. Then he blew air into them, and wound a rubber band round the end of each balloon.

The small twins tried every way they could think of to bounce the balloon on their noses. They jumped in the air, they got down on their knees, they even lay flat on the ground. Nothing worked.

Suddenly Flossie looked at the balloon man. "Did you ever try this?" she asked him.

The man grinned. "Sure."

"Please do it for us."

The man took both the blue and the yellow balloons, and tossed them into the air. As one came down, he knocked it high with his nose. Then before it started down again, he bounced the other one. Pretty soon he was making them go so fast that the twins could hardly keep track of the balloons.

When the man stopped, the children clapped. Freddie looked at him, and said, "I'll bet you worked in a circus."

The balloon man said Freddie was right. He had got tired of the job, and now he just sold balloons. Lots of children came to the zoo. Every day he sold dozens and dozens of balloons.

At once Freddie decided he wanted to be a balloon man when he grew up. Remembering what he had often heard his father say on the telephone when he was talking business, Freddie asked the man, "Is there much profit in such a deal?"

The balloon man laughed. He said there was enough profit to buy all the clothes and food he wanted for himself and his children. And what more could anyone ask?

The twins bought the yellow and blue balloons and took them back to the pool where the seals were. They tossed them into the water. The seals began to play with them.

The children did not want to go yet, but Mrs. Bobbsey came to say that the bus was leaving. They were going to make a stop at another part of the mountain to see something else.

The children said good-bye to the seals and followed their mother to the bus. When they had ridden about ten minutes, the driver stopped in front of a log cabin. Everyone got out and went inside.

The Bobbsey twins were disappointed.

"There's nothing in here but a lot of old souvenirs," Freddie grumbled. "Come on, Flossie, let's you and me go outside."

Flossie did not care about souvenirs any more than Freddie did. She followed him outdoors. Mrs. Bobbsey had not heard Freddie's remark and did not miss the children at once.

"Let's see what's behind the cabin," Freddie suggested.

In the woods back of the house was a dog kennel with a fenced-in yard. Several cunning puppies were playing in it.

"Oh, aren't they beeyootiful!" Flossie exclaimed. "Let's pet them."

The children ran up to the fence and leaned over. Each twin picked up a puppy.

The one in Freddie's arms squirmed hard to get away and finally did. Freddie tried to grab him. The puppy ran.

Freddie went after him, but he could not catch the smart little dog. Just as Freddie thought he was going to get hold of him, the puppy would twist and go a different way.

Flossie had put her little dog back in the yard. She ran after her twin. Suddenly Freddie lost his puppy completely. He stood under a big tree and called, "Come back here!"

At that instant Flossie screamed. A large, dark object was falling from high in the tree. It was going to land right on top of Freddie's head!

# CHAPTER XIII

## LITTLE HOOTY

FREDDIE moved just in time. The object hit his shoulder and fell to the grass.

"Freddie!" Flossie cried out. "Are you hurt?"

Her twin was so interested in looking at what had fallen to the ground that he did not answer.

On the grass lay a big bird's nest. Inside it was a fluffy gray mass of feathers with little black speckles. Up from the middle of the feathers shone two big brown eyes.

"Golly!" Freddie exclaimed. "What's that?"

"A bird, silly," his sister replied.

"But what kind?"

The question stumped Flossie. Never before had she seen a bird which had just feathers and two eyes like sour-ball candies.

"Maybe it's hurt," she said.

Freddie reached his hand into the nest. When he touched the bird, it fluttered frantically. Its wings spread out half the length of Freddie's arm and a sharp beak pecked at the boy.

"Watch out!" Flossie cried as her brother dropped the bird back in the nest.

"Ow!" Freddie exclaimed. "It's not hurt. It's just a bad bird."

Its big round eyes kept staring at the children, and the bird made a funny clicking noise with its beak.

"I wish we could take him with us," Freddie said.

"It'll bite your finger if you touch it," Flossie warned him.

Freddie thought for a second. Suddenly he saw a spreading branch that had been split from a tree, probably during a storm.

"Maybe I could carry it on this," he said, picking up the branch.

Freddie pushed the nest onto the branch. Then, with Flossie holding one side and Freddie the other, the twins walked back to the souvenir shop.

There was great excitement. Mrs. Bobbsey and the other bus passengers were searching for the missing twins. When they arrived, the bird caused still greater excitement.

"Gol-ly," said the bus driver, "it's an owl— a baby owl!"

"If the owl's only a baby," Flossie asked, "why does it bite people?"

The man explained that owls are strong from the time they are a few days old.

"This one is about two weeks old," he said.

He picked the bird up and felt its legs and wings carefully. They were not broken.

Suddenly Freddie put his face very close to the owl. *"Hoot hoot hoot!"* he said.

"What are you doing?" Flossie asked.

"Teaching Hooty Owl how to talk," Freddie answered.

*"Click click click!"* replied Hooty. His beak made a little snapping noise like a woodpecker's. It did not sound like talking.

"You couldn't talk when you were only two weeks old either, Freddie," Flossie giggled.

"What'll we do with Hooty?" the bus driver asked.

"Take him home," Freddie spoke up.

Mrs. Bobbsey shook her head. "The place for him is the zoo."

The children agreed, and the bus driver said he did not mind driving back there.

"Oh goodness gracious," said Flossie suddenly, "we didn't find the puppy!"

Freddie looked very guilty. His mother asked what the trouble was. The little boy hung his head and kicked at a pebble, but finally told her.

"What next!" Mrs. Bobbsey exclaimed.

She found the owner of the souvenir cabin and explained what had happened. Instead of looking worried, the man smiled and said, "We'll soon fix that."

He whistled, and a slender, long-eared, brown dog appeared from behind the cabin. The man said she was the lost puppy's mother.

"Pansy, go find your baby up in the woods," he told her.

The dog lifted her ears ever so slightly, then she ran back and forth sniffing the ground to get a scent. A few seconds later she bounded off into the woods.

"She's a hunting dog!" Freddie cried out.

Within three minutes they saw the mother dog coming back. In her jaws she held the lost puppy by the back of his neck.

"I knew Pansy would find her pup," the man said with a smile. "She's a good hunter."

The passengers were getting back into the bus for their return to the zoo, so the Bobbseys followed. The driver put the owl in its nest on the floor beside him.

When they reached the zoo, only the twins, their mother, and the driver got out. They found the keeper.

"We came back to give you an owl," Flossie said.

"His name's Hooty," Freddie explained, "but he can't hoot. He just clicks."

The bus driver handed the nest to the man.

"Well, I declare," the zoo keeper said. "I haven't seen a young 'un like this in a long, long time." The owl stared up and opened its beak. "Poor thing's hungry," said the man. "I'll give it some hamburger."

Flossie and Freddie grinned. Sometimes Dinah cooked hamburger for them, but they never knew baby owls would like it too.

The keeper went inside his house and returned in a moment with some chopped meat on a spoon. Hooty gobbled it up.

"He *was* hungry," Flossie said sympathetically. "Now can he have some milk?"

"Oh no," the zoo keeper said. "Baby owls can't have liquids. It makes them sick."

When he had fed Hooty, the keeper said he was very glad to have the bird, as there were no owls in his collection.

"By the way," he added, "right after you left, another boy came here wanting to know if I could take care of a bear."

After the Bobbseys got back on the bus, and were on the way home, Flossie said to her mother, "I wonder who the boy was."

Mrs. Bobbsey had no idea, but she was sure it had nothing to do with Kate.

When they arrived home, Dinah threw up her hands. "My, my," she said, "I thought you all had your lunch at the hotel. I'll fix something up real quick. Mr. Bobbsey and Bert didn't have time to finish their dessert."

"Why?" the twin's mother asked.

Dinah said there had been a big rumpus. Someone had come and said Kate had bitten a boy.

"And Mr. Bobbsey says we got to get rid of Kate right away," Dinah concluded.

"Oh dear, this is dreadful," said Mrs. Bobbsey.

She and the twins were so concerned that they could hardly eat. Just as they were finishing, Mr. Bobbsey returned. Flossie and Freddie ran to the porch to greet him. At this moment Nan, too, came back.

"Can't we keep Kate?" Freddie cried out.

"I'm afraid not," his father answered. "Kate's been cutting up."

"How?" Nan asked.

Mr. Bobbsey said that some children had been playing with the bear that morning and that Kate had scratched a boy named Gordon Bennett.

"Gordon's father sent for me," he continued, "and demanded that the bear be taken away."

"You're not going to do it, Dad!" Nan pleaded.

Tears filled her eyes. She was sure Kate would not hurt anybody.

While they were discussing the matter, Bert came racing back to the cabin. "I found him," he said to his father. "I made him own up!"

Bert explained that after Gordon's father had told them they could not keep the bear, Bert had gone to find Gordon. He did not like the boy and suspected there might be more to the story.

"Gordon was teasing Kate," Bert said hotly. "He admitted poking the bear with a long stick. When he came too close, Kate cuffed him with her paw. It was only a little scratch."

"Nevertheless, I'm afraid we're going to have more trouble," said Mr. Bobbsey. "We should take Kate some place where children can't annoy her."

"Let's build a wire fence around her," Bert suggested.

His father consented. Nan was overjoyed to hear that she could keep Kate, and promised to stay with her pet during the afternoon.

Bert told about meeting Danny Rugg in Westbrook, and the other twins were surprised. Bert also said he was sure now that Mr. Lincoln lived somewhere in the near-by woods.

Bert offered to go up to the hotel to see if they had any wire fencing to build an enclosure for Kate. Nan and Flossie went out to give the bear some sugar cookies, meat, and a handful of lettuce. The bear ate the food and then stood on her head without being asked.

"She's thanking you for feeding her," Flossie giggled.

This put an idea into the little girl's head. After the Bobbseys had eaten their supper that evening, Flossie placed a cushion in the middle of the living-room floor. She put her hands on the floor, her head on the cushion, and slowly raised herself into the air.

"Huh!" Freddie exclaimed. "I can do that, too." And he did.

Nan laughed. "Mother," she said, "Flossie and Freddie are thanking you for dinner, just the way Kate did."

The children played a little longer, then went to bed. When Nan awoke next morning, she ran to her window to look at Kate. The bear was not there! Nan rushed from the room, almost colliding with her mother.

"Mother, where's Kate?" she cried out.

Mrs. Bobbsey put her arm around Nan.

"Kate's gone," she said sadly. "She disappeared last night."

# CHAPTER XIV

## A MEAN TRICK

"I'M GOING to find Kate!" Nan cried.

When the other children heard the sad news, they too wanted to help find the bear. The twins began their search directly after breakfast.

First Bert went over to the tree where Kate had been tied. There was no trace of the rope nor of the chain.

"If Kate gnawed through the rope," Bert reasoned, "some of it would be left on the tree. Kate was untied by somebody!"

The question was: Who? Maybe Mr. Lincoln himself had come.

"I'll bet Gordon had something to do with it," Bert guessed. "Let's ask him."

"We'd better look around here first," Nan advised.

She and Bert looked for tracks but could find none because the ground was so hard. Next they asked people in the neighboring cabins about Kate. None of them had seen her taken away. Finally the twins came to Gordon's house. When they reached it, they found Gordon playing roughly with a cat.

He was throwing her into the air to see if she could land on her feet. The cat yowled every time she was tossed up, but would twist her back and always land on her feet.

"Don't do that," Nan called out to Gordon. "You'll hurt the cat's back."

"Why don't you play with your bear and mind your own business?" came the reply.

Just then the boy let out a yell and dropped the cat. While he had been talking, the cat had scratched his hand and run away. The Bobbsey twins laughed, for it had served Gordon right.

"Why don't you pests go home?" Gordon said angrily.

"We came to ask you if you had seen Kate," Bert said.

"No, I haven't," Gordon replied.

Something about the way he said it, and a certain look in his eye, made Bert suspicious.

"You'd better tell me the truth," Bert told him.

"Is that so? Think you're smart, don't you?" Gordon started to laugh. "Well, run along twinsy-winsies. You won't find out anything from me." Gordon went into the cabin.

"Gee," said Bert, as he and Nan started off, "if I had a disposition like that, I'd jump into the river! Well, what'll we do now?"

Nan thought they should go ask the zoo keeper more about the boy who had wanted to leave a bear with him.

"Good idea," said Bert.

He and Nan took a bus to the zoo and found the owner. They told him they were Freddie and Flossie's older brother and sister. They said Kate was gone, and asked what the boy who had spoken about a bear the day before looked like.

"Two sets of twins in one family!" the man exclaimed. "I'm sorry to hear about your bear," he added sympathetically. "Now, about that boy yesterday." The man looked at Bert. "About your age, a little bigger. I hardly noticed what he looked like."

Bert and Nan were disappointed. "Didn't you notice *anything* about him?" Bert prodded.

"Nothing except the baseball cap he wore. It said *Lakeport Juniors* on it."

"Oh boy!" Bert exclaimed. "That's a wonderful clue, sir."

"You think it was Danny Rugg?" Nan asked her twin excitedly.

"I'll bet anything it was," Bert replied. "Come on, we're going to Red Ridge Lodge!"

They thanked the man and asked directions to the hotel. It was only a fifteen-minute walk, so the twins hiked to the place. As they went up the front steps, they met Mrs. Rugg.

"How do you do, Mrs. Rugg," Nan and Bert said together, and Bert added, "We'd like to see Danny. Do you know where he is?"

"Danny's out back of the hotel playing baseball," she replied.

The children hurried to the baseball diamond. A game of softball was going on among the boys. Danny was playing in center field.

"There he is," Nan said, looking over a low wire fence.

"Let's not bother him till the game's over," Bert advised.

Just then the boy at bat gave the ball a hard crack. It sailed high into the air, directly toward Danny's position.

"If Danny doesn't run back to get it," Bert told Nan, "it's going to be a home run!"

Danny did not move until he heard the other players shouting. Then he saw the soaring ball and tried to run back for the catch. But it was too late. The ball cleared the fence by two inches, and Bert caught it neatly.

The players shouted and threw their caps into the air as the batter ran around the bases. Then the boys hurried out to the fence, where Danny was storming over to Bert.

"Keep your hands off the ball!" Danny shouted.

"I didn't touch it till it was over the fence," Bert defended himself.

"I don't care," Danny cried angrily, shaking his fist. "You made me miss the catch."

By this time the umpire and the other players had come up to Bert and Nan.

"This boy didn't interfere with your catch," the umpire said.

The captain of Danny's team agreed. "If you'd been on the beam, you could have had that one," he scolded. "You've been making bone-head plays all morning."

The captain turned to Bert. "How would you like to play center field next inning?"

Bert grinned. "That would be swell. Thanks."

Danny's face became red with rage. "You can't put me out of the game," he stormed.

"I'm not putting you out," the captain said. "I'm replacing you for the last two innings."

Bert felt like asking Danny at once about Kate, but he had promised to play the rest of the game and did not want to delay it.

Nan walked over to where the spectators were. Bert got right into the game while Danny sat scowling on the players' bench.

"I can hit better'n Bert Bobbsey any day," he muttered.

But the other boys did not think so. Bert hit a two-bagger and caught two fly balls for outs to help the team win the game.

When it was over, his new-found teammates slapped him on the back and invited him to come over and play at Red Ridge Lodge any time.

This made Danny angrier than ever. He strode over to Bert. "Stay away from Red Ridge!" he ordered.

"I wouldn't have come here at all, except to find out about our bear," Bert retorted. "What did you do with her?"

Danny looked frightened. "I wouldn't tell you even if I knew," he said. "Now go back to your old hotel and stay there!"

With that he gave Bert a shove. Bert shoved him right back. Danny teetered over a bat lying on the grass behind him. His legs shot out from under him and he landed in the dust.

The other players laughed. Danny got up and gritted his teeth. His eyes blazed.

"I'll get even with you for this!" he shouted at Bert.

# CHAPTER XV

## THE RESCUE BEAR

THE BASEBALL players, who were sitting on the bench with Danny, expected a fight. Bert Bobbsey was ready. But Danny suddenly changed his mind and ran toward the lodge.

"He's a sissy," one of the boys called out.

Bert ran after Danny. "What did you do with our bear?" he demanded.

Danny ran even faster and did not answer. In a moment, he bounded up the steps of the lodge porch and hurried inside. This did not stop Bert.

"You're going to tell me," he said, catching up.

Danny looked around for a place to go. Unfortunately for him, he had run into a corner of the lobby. Now he could not escape.

Bert asked him again what he had done with Kate. Danny started to say something, then stopped.

"You may as well own up," said Bert. "A man told us about you."

"How'd he know?" Danny asked sullenly.

"By your baseball cap."

Danny hung his head. "I was only playing a joke on you," he said. "I got halfway here and then I couldn't hold Kate. She ran away in the woods."

"You came to Rainbow House last night and took Kate all by yourself?" Bert asked, astounded.

"I'm not telling you any more," said Danny. "Bears shouldn't be chained up anyway," he defended himself.

Bert knew the bear could take care of herself so long as people were kind to her. If a hunter came along, however, there was no telling what might happen.

Bert was worried. He decided to get some of the other boys from Red Ridge Lodge to help him search the woods. Nan wanted to go along, too.

The team captain invited the twins to stay to luncheon. Then about two-thirty they set out with four other boys. They hiked for a long time, whistling for the bear. Nan kept calling, "Kate! Kate!" every few minutes, but the friendly black bear did not appear.

Finally the group came to a little cottage among the trees. A woman was sitting on the porch, knitting. Bert went up to her and asked if she had seen the bear. She said no, and then asked where Bert was staying.

When he told her, she said she had a friend who was staying at Rainbow House. "Her name is Mrs. Bennington."

"Oh, she lives right next door to us," said Bert. "I slept outside her cottage the night I tried to catch the ghost."

"Ghost?" the woman said.

Nan explained about the mysterious person who made beautiful baskets and left them in exchange for food. "But he hasn't been around lately," she said.

The woman smiled. "Maybe that's because he's been visiting this part of the mountain," she said.

The twins were very attentive as the woman told more about it. They learned that the mysterious person's method had been the same at both places.

"How long ago was he here?" Bert asked.

"He came last night. He asked only for groceries and milk, but I left him an apple pie, too."

"We have something we think belongs to him," Bert said. "We didn't want to leave it in the ghost's basket until we were sure he's Mr. Lincoln."

"So his name is Mr. Lincoln?" the woman

said. "Well, if I should ever see him, I'll tell him what you said. What's your name?"

The twins told her, then said good-bye to their new friend and went on looking for Kate. They had gone only a short distance when Nan saw something move behind some berry bushes. She watched intently to see what it might be.

Suddenly she exclaimed, "Bert! I think I see a man. He might be Mr. Lincoln!"

Bert left the other boys and followed his sister. The person had disappeared, but they could hear running footsteps. From some spot near by came a loud grunt, followed by a growl. Nan and Bert stopped and looked around. A moment later a large, black mass came from behind a tree and faced them.

"Kate!" Nan cried out.

She ran forward and hugged the old bear. "Oh, I'm so glad we found you," she said.

Kate was glad to see her young mistress, too, and promptly stood on her head. By this time the other ballplayers had run up. They were amazed to see what was going on. Bert advised them not to touch the bear until she got used to them.

"She's all right after she knows you," he said.

Suddenly the twins remembered that they had been chasing someone in the woods. Bert asked two of the boys to stay with Nan and Kate. He and the other fellows would try to find the person who had run away.

It was easy to follow the man's trail, because he had crushed the grass here and there with his heavy boots, and broken low bushes in his path.

Presently the boys came to a brook. Here the man's footprints ended. Bert and the others waded across the stream, and searched the opposite bank. But they could find no more tracks.

Disappointed, they turned around and went back to where Nan was waiting with Kate and the two boys.

"I'd love to take Kate back with us," Nan said slowly. "But maybe it *is* cruel to chain her up."

"Tell you what," said Bert. "Why don't we let Kate decide for herself?"

"All right," Nan agreed.

The children started back for Red Ridge Lodge. Nan looked back over her shoulder. Kate had sat down and was looking after them. Nan was sure the old bear had a sad look in her eyes. Turning around, she called back:

"You can come with us if you want to!"

The invitation was all Kate needed. She got up and waddled after the children.

"Oh, she's coming!" Nan cried excitedly.

Bert was as happy as his twin. The other boys

were pretty envious. Everyone wished he might have the bear for a pet.

"We'll be over to see you," one of them spoke up. "Say, why don't the fellows at Rainbow House get up a ball team? Then we'll play you."

"That's an idea!" Bert agreed enthusiastically.

Just as he said this, old Kate stopped walking. Nan coaxed her to go on and Bert shoved. The bear refused to move.

"What's the matter with her?" the captain asked.

The twins could not figure it out. Sighing, they trailed along behind the boys.

Kate grunted and growled.

"She's trying to tell us something," Nan decided. "I'm going back."

She and Bert turned around. As they did so, Kate got up and started off through the woods in another direction from the one they had been taking.

"I'll bet she wants us to follow her," Nan said. "What'll we do?"

"You wait here a minute," her twin answered.

He ran to the other boys, and told them what had happened. They, too, turned back. Kate was still ambling along in the direction she had chosen. The children followed.

"Oh, I've got it!" said Bert suddenly. "This is a straight line to Rainbow House. Kate's leading us home!"

"That's right," one of the ballplayers spoke up. "You don't have to go back to Red Ridge Lodge from here. You can cut across the river."

"The river?" Nan repeated. She looked worried. "We mustn't go any farther. It's too dangerous!"

# CHAPTER XVI

## CAPTAIN BOBBSEY

"WHAT do you mean, too dangerous?" one of the boys asked in surprise.

Nan told about the cliff with the loose rocks on the side of Rainbow Falls toward which they were heading.

"No wonder nobody ever goes there," another boy spoke up. "We didn't know it was as dangerous as that."

Suddenly Kate took a right-angle turn. "She knows what she's doing," the first boy laughed. "Your bear's going to follow the river till she finds a safe place to cross. She's smart."

Ten minutes later Kate led them downhill to a spot where the river widened.

"This is a shallow place," one of the Red Ridge ballplayers said. "You can walk across here. It's about half a mile from Rainbow House. Well, so long. And don't forget about the team, Bert."

"I won't."

Bidding the boys good-bye, Bert and Nan took off their shoes and socks and waded across. Kate splashed ahead of them.

As the twins followed along the pebbly shore, they talked about the fleeing figure they had seen in the woods.

"He couldn't have been Mr. Lincoln, or Kate wouldn't have come to us," Nan remarked.

"Maybe he was Mr. Smink looking for another secret trail. Say, you don't suppose *he* could be the ghost?"

Nan was startled by this idea. "You mean he lives in these woods? But what about the baskets?"

"He probably steals 'em from Mr. Lincoln's place," her twin suggested.

All this time the twins had been getting closer to Rainbow Falls.

"Listen," Bert whispered, "I think I hear the singing!"

The twins stood still. Even Kate stopped and cocked her head, as if she were listening, too. Then suddenly the beautiful voice burst into song.

Kate had been sitting on her haunches. Now she suddenly got up and began running around in circles.

"What's the matter?" Nan asked her.

"The singing's making Kate excited," Nan said.

"You're right!" Bert burst out. "Maybe she knows the secret of Rainbow Falls!"

The singing stopped and Kate quieted down. The children's eyes roved the woodland at the top of the cliff, but they could see no one. At last the twins started off again, soon arriving at their cabin.

"Mother, they're back with Kate!" Flossie cried out gleefully.

Mr. and Mrs. Bobbsey, the little twins, and Dinah were astounded.

"Where'd you find her?" Freddie demanded.

"Who took her? How'd you bring her back?" Flossie wanted to know.

"She brought *us*," Nan laughed. "Kate wanted to come back."

While Bert tied Kate to the tree in back of the cabin, Nan began the story of their adventure. It lasted far into the evening, with the little twins asking, "And what happened next?" every time Bert or Nan finished part of the tale.

When it was time to go to bed, Flossie went out to hug Kate and tell her how glad she was to have her back.

Before the children had finished breakfast next morning, their playmates from the other cabins were outside, calling for them. They had seen Kate and wanted to know how the Bobbseys had found her.

The twins told the story all over again. Then Bert took some of the boys aside and asked if they would like to form a baseball team, to play the boys at Red Ridge Lodge. They all liked the idea, and asked Bert to be captain.

"Only we haven't enough players," one of them said. Only seven boys were present.

"How about Gordon?" Bert suggested.

The other boys made faces when Gordon's name was mentioned.

"I think we should give Gordon a chance," Bert insisted. "I saw him catching fly balls. He's pretty good."

One of the boys was sent to call Gordon. Bert went for a softball and bat, and the players headed for the Rainbow House diamond. Gordon came running over to join them.

"We're getting up a ball team," said Bert. "How'd you like to play on it?"

"Don't see how you can get along without me," Gordon smirked.

Bert ignored him. "We still need one more player," he said. "What'll we do?"

All the boys thought. There were some small boys at the resort and a few who were a lot older. But there seemed to be no more about their own age.

"I know," Nan said. She had come over to watch her brother practice and had heard the conversation. "You can get a girl player."

"Oh phooey!" Gordon exclaimed in disgust.

"You mean *you* want to play, Nan?" Bert asked his sister.

Nan laughed. "No, but I had lunch the day before yesterday with a girl who won a medal for playing softball."

The other players thought it was a joke and laughed. But Bert knew his sister.

"Go get her," he suggested. "At least we can try her out, fellows. We want to have a team."

While Nan ran off toward the hotel, the boys practiced throwing the ball and hitting a few high ones for the fielders to catch. In a few minutes Nan returned with a girl with dark-red, short hair and freckles.

"This is Sarah Willets," Nan said, introducing her. "She would like to play on your team."

Sarah smiled and took a hitch in the belt which held up her blue shorts.

"May I be pitcher?" she asked.

The boys looked at one another.

"Ever pitch before?" Gordon snapped.

"Sure." Sarah smiled.

"Well, pitch a couple to me," Gordon ordered. The boy wanted to hit the ball so far that nobody would want Sarah on the team.

Bert tossed the ball to Sarah while Gordon put a bat over his shoulder.

"All right. Let's have it," Gordon commanded with a sneer.

Sarah was a left-handed pitcher. She wound up and threw the ball toward Gordon. It came very fast; so fast that Gordon swung and missed it. The other boys and Nan cheered Sarah.

"Anybody can be lucky," Gordon pouted.

Sarah threw again. This time Gordon got a foul ball.

"That's strike two," Nan cried.

"Oh, be quiet," Gordon scowled.

Sarah threw the next ball as if it were going to be very fast. But instead, the ball went slowly toward the batter. Gordon swung at it long before it got to him, and missed it.

"Strike three! You're out!" Bert shouted.

"No, I'm not," Gordon retorted. "I tipped it. It's a foul ball."

The other boys knew that Gordon was just making up an excuse. He had not even touched the ball. Before Gordon could say any more, Bert walked up to Sarah.

"You're on our team," he said, "if the other fellows want you."

"We sure do!" they chorused.

Gordon did not say a word. He was so angry that he picked up the ball and tossed it into the air. As it came down, he whacked it with his bat. The ball sailed over the field.

Suddenly Nan cried out in alarm. Across the field lumbered her bear. The ball was headed straight for Kate's head!

It landed hard on her nose. She let out a howl of pain. Several children standing around the field screamed.

Kate growled and started for Gordon.

"Run!" one of the ballplayers shouted.

Gordon took to his heels, but it was amazing how fast the angry bear could go.

# CHAPTER XVII

## FREDDIE IN A RACE

CHILDREN scattered in every direction. The only ones who stayed near the angry bear were Nan and Bert. They kept calling to her to stop, but she paid no attention.

"Oh dear, what'll we do?" Nan called to Bert.

Bert himself wondered what to do. He could not seem to think of anything. Gordon's father, who had been on the hotel porch and had seen what happened, ran out and picked up a bat. He raced toward Kate.

"Oh, please don't hurt her!" Nan pleaded.

"You'll only make her madder!" Bert yelled.

Gordon's father paid no attention to the Bobbseys' plea. He hit the bear hard on the rump and told her to halt.

The bear lifted her upper lip, showing her great teeth. She let out another growl, and turned on Mr. Bennett. The man jumped out of the way and sped toward the hotel, which his son had now reached.

119

Nan and Bert were in a panic. They were sure Mr. Bennett would call the police and Kate would be shot.

"We must do something!" Bert cried.

"I have an idea!" Nan gasped. She stopped running, and called sharply, "Up, Kate!"

The bear heard the familiar command and slowed down a bit. Nan was hopeful, and repeated, "Up, Kate!"

It was plain to see that Kate was now a puzzled bear. She was still angry with Gordon and his father. On the other hand, she was very fond of Nan and wished to heed that kind, familiar voice. Finally the old bear stopped and sat back on her haunches. The twins ran up to her. Bert patted Kate gently, while Nan hugged her.

"I'll fix your nose so it won't hurt so much," she offered. "Please come back to the cabin."

Nan took hold of the chain. Kate seemed willing to go along with her young mistress. Bert went to tell Mr. Bennett that it would not be necessary to get the police now.

When Nan reached the house, she tied Kate and went for some salve. As she daubed it on the bear's nose, she noticed that the hook to which Kate had been tied was badly bent. Probably Kate had become lonesome and broken away herself.

"Where are Freddie and Flossie?" Mrs. Bobbsey asked, worried. "Are they all right?"

"Oh, Kate didn't hurt anyone," Nan said.

Soon Bert arrived with several boys to help build a wire enclosure for the bear. She did not like the idea at all, and whimpered each time Nan came near her.

"I'm terribly sorry," the girl said. "Never mind, Kate, we'll have fun tomorrow."

The hobby show was scheduled for the following afternoon. Suddenly Nan had a frightening thought. After what had happened, maybe they would not let Kate perform!

"What do you think, Mother?" Nan asked her.

Mrs. Bobbsey was doubtful, too. She said people probably would be afraid of Kate now.

"But why don't you ask the hostess?" she suggested.

Nan went to the hotel to see Mrs. Nixon, and find out what to do about it. The young woman in turn went to the manager. At first he was inclined to say no. At last, however, he said that if both Bert and Nan would hold onto the bear, and if Mr. Bobbsey would stay with them, he would permit the performance.

"Oh, thank you very much," Nan said, and hurried back to the cabin.

When three o'clock arrived the next day, the

whole Bobbsey family walked up to the hotel, with Kate in tow. Mr. and Mrs. Bobbsey and the older twins took turns staying with her, while the others went into the hotel to look at the children's exhibits.

There were wooden canoes, leather belts, and copper flower bowls which the boys and girls had made in the craft shop. A little girl played a musical saw. A boy did tricks with handkerchiefs and cards.

Mrs. Nixon had arranged outdoor games for the children who did not have anything to exhibit. The afternoon was to end with Kate's performance.

A whistle blew, and the small children hurried out to the play field. The first game was a sack race.

It was fun to see Freddie and Flossie and other children their age trying to run with potato sacks tied over their feet. Freddie almost won this race, but near the end he fell down and was disqualified. Flossie did win it, and received a little sailboat for a prize.

Freddie was a bit envious. He declared he would win the next race, and he hoped the prize would be a boat also.

The next event was not a race, but a game of

tag. The Bobbsey twins had never played this kind of tag. Three children were in it at one time. A runner was chosen to try to tag seven trees before the other two runners could tag him.

The young children found this very hard to do. One by one they were out of the game. Finally only Freddie and two other little boys were left. Freddie was "It."

The little Bobbsey boy had watched the other players carefully. He had noticed that when they ran in a straight line, they had always been tagged out.

"I'll go in and out among the trees," he decided.

When the whistle blew, he started off. As he neared the first tree, Mrs. Nixon gave the signal for the other two runners to go after him.

Freddie touched the first tree quickly and raced toward the second. The other two boys were not far behind him. Freddie dodged in back of the second tree as he tagged it, and ran to the third. The runners behind him dodged back of the tree also and sped after Freddie.

Just before reaching the third tree, Freddie ran out in front of it, tagged it, and dashed on to the fourth. The two boys behind him became confused. They did not know as they came to each tree whether Freddie would go in front of it or in back of it.

As Freddie neared the last tree—and he had not been tagged out yet—Nan and Bert began to jump up and down.

"Hurry!" they cried out. "Faster!"

Freddie had never run faster in his life. The other two boys had caught onto his little scheme, and were pounding after him.

*Freddie just made it!*

"He won! He won!" Nan screamed. She was so thrilled that she almost let go of Kate.

All the Bobbseys were pleased that Freddie had come out first in the tag game. When he ran back to Mrs. Nixon, she smiled and congratulated him. She had overheard his wish for a sailboat, and said that he, too, might have one for a prize.

Freddie was so excited to hear this that he almost forgot to be in the next race. It was to be an egg race, and four children were competing at once. Flossie and Freddie were in the last group.

It was difficult to pick up the hard-boiled eggs on a teaspoon and walk with them to the starting point. The children dropped them several times.

When Freddie had only two more eggs to collect, Gordon Bennett walked out on the field.

As if by accident, he kicked one of the eggs out of place.

Quickly he leaned down, picked it up, and stepped back to put the egg in place. As Freddie came running up to get it, the older boy cried out, "Look out you don't drop that egg, Freddie!"

Freddie was having a bad enough time as it was. Hearing this, he became nervous. The little boy managed to get the egg onto the spoon, but as he lifted it up, the egg wobbled dangerously.

Freddie juggled it. The egg just did not want to stay on the spoon.

Gordon laughed loudly. This unnerved Freddie. He raised his arm and the egg flew out of his hand.

Unexpectedly it landed on top of Gordon's head, and the shell broke. To Freddie's utter bewilderment, gooey, yellow liquid ran down Gordon's face. The egg was not hard-boiled!

Gordon had substituted a fresh egg for the one he had kicked out of line, hoping to play a trick on Freddie Bobbsey. The trick had turned back on himself!

"Oh, he looks awful funny," Flossie shrieked, as Gordon stormed off, with everyone laughing.

In a little while the games were over. Then Nan put on her performance with Kate. The people at the hotel who had not seen the bear perform thought it was wonderful what Nan could make her do.

Kate had a surprise even for Nan. As the show ended and everyone clapped, the bear sat back on her haunches and clapped, too!

The Bobbsey twins had had a wonderful time at the hobby show. But when they trooped into the cabin, Dinah met them with a worried look on her face.

"I'm afraid I've got bad news for you children," she said.

## CHAPTER XVIII

### TWIN DETECTIVES

"BAD NEWS?" Nan asked. "What is it, Dinah?"

"It's goin' to make you feel very bad," she said, drawing a paper from her apron pocket. She handed it to Nan.

It was a piece of white writing paper folded in two. Nan opened it. On the inside was printed a crude-looking note. It said:

*Leave food and knife. Let Kate go.*

"Where did you find this?" Bert asked.

"In this basket," Dinah replied. "It was on the porch."

She held a woven basket toward the boy. It was the same kind that had been left before.

"The ghost!" Freddie exclaimed in awe.

"Oh dear," Flossie sighed. "Poor Kate will have to go live with a ghost. Maybe she'll turn into a ghost bear."

The others laughed, but Bert was puzzled by the whole thing. Finally he called Nan aside.

"I think the note is a fake," he said. "The ghost never came around in the daytime before."

"That's right," Nan agreed.

"And if the ghost wants Kate, why doesn't he take her himself instead of asking us to let her go?"

This sounded reasonable to Nan. If the ghost, Mr. Lincoln, or whoever the mysterious person was, wanted his pet, he would not ask anyone to let her loose to roam in the woods.

"I think somebody's playing a joke on us," Bert declared.

"Who?"

Bert was not sure. The most likely person was Danny Rugg, of course. He would want to get square with Bert because of the softball episode.

"What I can't understand is how he knew about Mr. Lincoln's knife," the boy said. "I didn't tell him."

Nan asked who did know about it beside the Bobbseys. Bert thought hard. There was the boat salesman at the Sportsman's Show at Lakeport. Another person was the friend of Mrs. Bennington over near Red Ridge Lodge. There also were a few store clerks in Westbrook who knew, too.

"Danny might have found out from one of them," Nan suggested.

"Yes, he could have," Bert agreed with a faraway look in his eyes. He sat down on the porch steps and put his chin in his hands. "You know, Nan," he said, "I'll bet Danny's got a friend here at Rainbow House."

"What makes you think that?" his twin asked.

Bert said it was a good distance from one hotel to the other. It was unlikely that Danny's parents would let him come over unless he knew someone at Rainbow House. Bert snapped his fingers.

"I'll bet it's Gordon Bennett!" he said. "You remember Gordon acted as if he knew who let Kate loose."

"How could we find out?" Nan asked her twin.

"Let's keep an eye on Gordon," Bert proposed. "He's probably going to meet Danny tonight."

The twins talked the plan over with their parents. Mr. Bobbsey thought Bert probably was right about the note being a hoax. He said the printing was quite different from that in Mrs. Bennington's note, which he had seen.

"I can tell you something else, too," the twins' father added. "This morning I went up to the hotel to use the phone. Gordon was just saying good-bye to someone named Danny."

"Oh boy, that settles it!" Bert cried gleefully. "Either Danny or Gordon left the note!"

After supper the older twins got a flashlight and set off for Gordon's house. They found him walking up and down the trail in front of his cabin.

"Hi!" Bert said as they approached him.

"Hi," Gordon said without enthusiasm.

"Nice evening for a basket picnic," Bert grinned.

Gordon looked at them out of the corner of his eye. "Nobody's going on a picnic," he said.

"Where *are* you going?" Nan asked.

Gordon seemed embarrassed. "Why, uh, I wasn't going anywhere."

He walked away from them, but Bert and Nan followed.

"Hey, what is this?" Gordon said, annoyed. "You two think you're detectives?"

"Oh no," Bert said breezily. "We just want to take a walk with you."

"I don't want you to. Go on home," Gordon ordered.

He walked fast up the trail. Bert and Nan kept right with him. Gordon slowed down. The twins did. too.

"All right!" Gordon shouted at them. "If you must know, I'm going to visit a friend at the hotel. Now scram!"

"We'll see that you get there safely," Bert said, trying not to laugh.

Gordon was bursting with anger, but he tightened his lips and walked to the hotel as fast as he could. When he got there, he ran up the front steps two at a time. As he disappeared into the lobby, Sarah Willetts came out.

"Oh, hello, Sarah," Nan called.

"Hello, Nan. Hello, Bert."

Nan told Sarah they were keeping an eye on Gordon. "He says he's going to visit a friend in the hotel," Bert added, "but we don't believe him. I think he'll try to sneak out one of the other doors."

"That'll be easy to find out," Sarah said, chuckling. She did not like Gordon either. "There are only three doors and we can each stand at one of them."

"Swell," Bert said. "Whoever sees him first, whistle."

When Gordon went inside Rainbow House, he waited a few minutes. Then he stepped cautiously to the side door and peeked out. There was Nan standing outside. He tried the front entrance. Bert was waiting there.

"I'll fool 'em," he thought. "I'll use the back door."

Gordon went out the back way. Nobody was standing there but the girl baseball player. He held his head high and walked past her.

Suddenly Sarah whistled. Gordon was startled to hear a girl whistle so loudly. As he stared at her, Nan and Bert Bobbsey came running up.

"We thought you were visiting a friend," Bert said, grinning.

"I—I was, but he wasn't in," Gordon said. "Anyhow, it's none of your business. Now go away and leave me alone."

Nan and Bert said good-bye to Sarah and hurried after Gordon. The boy walked to the woods. Suddenly Bert thought he saw a shadow behind a big pine tree.

"Well, here's where we leave you," he told Gordon. Bert gave his sister's hand a squeeze to let her know he had another plan in mind.

"Good riddance," Gordon grumbled as he strode off toward the pine tree.

Bert and Nan walked out of sight, then retraced their steps and hid behind a bush. In the dimness of the woods, they saw Danny Rugg come from behind the pine tree and talk with Gordon.

"There they are now!" Bert whispered to

Nan. "I'll bet they'll go straight to our cabin as soon as it's dark."

In a few minutes the two boys started off. The Bobbseys followed them, careful not to let themselves be seen. But the path that Danny and Gordon took did not lead to the twins' cabin. It went in the opposite direction.

Suddenly Bert stopped short. "Nan," he whispered, "maybe Danny and Gordon didn't write that note after all."

The awful thought had come to Bert that perhaps at this very moment somebody else was stealing their bear!

# CHAPTER XIX

## THE INDIAN TRAIL

"WHY DON'T you go home and watch the house?" Bert suggested to Nan. "I'll follow the boys."

"All right, but don't get lost," she begged her twin. "You keep the flashlight."

The light was almost gone. Nan hurried. Once she missed the path, and felt a little frightened, but finally she reached the cabin.

Rushing to the rear, Nan was relieved to find Kate there in her wire enclosure. She was asleep. Freddie and Flossie had gone to bed, and Mr. and Mrs. Bobbsey were attending a party at one of the neighboring cabins.

Nan told Dinah what had happened, and asked her to watch outside with her. First she wrote a note, saying that they had the lost property of Mr. Lincoln. If he wanted it, *please* knock on the door. She put the note into the basket. Then she and Dinah went out among the trees, watching to see if anyone would come.

They talked a little, in whispered tones. Nan began to grow sleepy, and Dinah suggested that she go to bed. The faithful cook said she would watch, at least until Mr. and Mrs. Bobbsey returned from the party.

"Oh, I want to wait until Bert gets back," said Nan.

Dinah was worried about Bert. She went into the kitchen and looked at the clock. An hour had passed since Nan's return!

"I don't like this," said Dinah, when she came outside again. "Bert's all by himself in the woods. He might be lost."

Nan began to worry, too. Bert might even have had a fight with Danny and Gordon, and been hurt.

Another fifteen minutes went by. Dinah said she could stand it no longer. She was going to get in touch with Mr. Bobbsey.

In the meantime, Bert had quietly trailed the other two boys. They had gone farther and farther from the Bobbsey cabin. Bert could not understand what they were doing.

Presently Gordon stopped, and the two sat down on the stump of a tree. It was pretty dark by this time. In a moment an argument started.

"You sure muffed everything," said Danny. "Why'd you have to let those Bobbsey twins follow you?"

"I couldn't help it," Gordon whined. "I tried to get rid of 'em. I think they know we left the basket and the note."

Bert grinned.

"Everything's spoiled now," said Danny. "I'd better not stay all night with you. The Bobbseys might see me."

"How about trying our other trick tomorrow night?" Gordon proposed.

"I don't know if I can get away," Danny replied. "I'll let you know."

Were they going to say what the trick was, Bert wondered? He listened very carefully, but they did not say a word to give him a clue.

Finally Danny stood up. "Walk to the bus with me, will you?" he asked Gordon.

"Sure. I never have to be home any special time," Gordon bragged.

They stood up and walked along the path. Bert started to follow. Then, hearing the roar of the waterfall, he suddenly realized where he was. By going down toward it, he could get home more quickly.

As Bert came to the falls, he stopped short.

His heart began to beat fast. His spine prickled.

Ahead of him was a beautiful, but frightening sight. It was dark all around him. But there was a light shining through the falls!

A moment later Bert heard the strange, lovely singing which the twins had heard before. It seemed to come from the lighted water.

"There *must* be a ghost on the mountain!" Bert told himself nervously.

He was too fascinated to leave the spot. The water remained aglow for several minutes, then there was complete darkness.

The singing continued. Now Bert did not think the voice came from the water. It seemed to be somewhere up and beyond the falls.

"But how could anybody get up there?" the boy asked himself.

The singing suddenly stopped. Bert waited a long time. Neither the light nor the voice came again, so the boy started for home.

As he came toward the cabin, with his bobbing flashlight in front of him, Nan rushed toward her brother.

"Oh, I'm so glad you're back!" she cried. "Dinah's gone to get Daddy and Mother."

"We better stop her," Bert advised. "No point in scaring them."

They dashed after the cook and reached her

just as she got to the neighbor's cabin. Bert told her and Nan what he had found out, and how the waterfall had looked.

"Let's go up to the hotel tomorrow morning and see if anybody knows about it," Nan suggested.

Both children were tired and did not argue when Dinah insisted that they go to bed.

"So the whole thing was a joke," said the twins' father at breakfast the next morning, "but not my idea of a very funny one." Then, turning to the small twins, he asked, "And what are my Fat Fairy and my Little Fireman going to do today?"

Flossie and Freddie wanted to go down to the waterfall and dig again for the pot of gold. They also hoped to sail the new boats they had received at the hobby show. Dinah said she would go with them.

"And how about you two?" Mr. Bobbsey asked Bert and Nan.

Bert said they were going to inquire at the hotel if anyone knew about the light or the singing at the waterfall. He and Nan went off together but learned nothing. No one had ever noticed the strange light nor the singing; not even Possum, who had lived in the vicinity all his life. This gave Bert another idea.

"Say, Possum," Bert asked, "do you know any secret trails around here? I learned about them from a magazine. Maybe we could find out about the singing that way."

"Sure I know some secret trails," Possum said. "Want me to show you one?"

"That would be swell," Bert answered. "When could you go?"

Possum said this was his day off, and he could take them about eleven o'clock. The Bobbseys were thrilled.

"Why don't we have a picnic?" Nan suggested. "I'll run home and ask Mother."

"Put on rubber-soled shoes," Possum directed. "It'll be slippery where we're going."

The twins hurried to the cabin. Mrs. Bobbsey gave permission for the trip, and Dinah packed a lunch while they changed their clothes. When Bert and Nan met Possum again, they hardly recognized him. He was dressed like a hunter!

Grinning at them, he said, "All ready!" and led the way. First they went down the wooded hill to the river and crossed at the spot where the children had come over before. Instead of following the trail the old bear had taken, Possum struck out through the bushes.

"Is this a secret trail?" Nan asked him. "How can you tell?"

Possum laughed. "If I should tell you, it wouldn't be secret, would it? Well, this is how I figure it. Indians always used a lot of sense doing things. I figure the Indians came on down to the river through the cave and along here. I'll show you."

In a few minutes he started to scramble up a pile of rocks. The twins climbed up, too. At the top Possum said, "Here's the opening to the cave. Too small for the summer visitors to bother with. Think you can make it?"

The twins had to lie flat on their stomachs to look inside. It was pitch black.

"Sure, we can make it," Bert declared.

"Is it safe?" Nan asked.

Possum pulled a flashlight from his pocket. "Just watch your step and you'll be all right. Follow me."

He got down and inched his way through the opening. Bert and Nan pulled themselves along on their elbows. The passageway to the cave was about five feet long.

Finally Possum stood up and turned on his flashlight. It revealed a cave as big as a good-sized room. But how different from the usual room! Everywhere along the walls were shiny rocks in all kinds of patterns.

"How beautiful!" Nan exclaimed. "It's like —like a stage for a fairy play!"

"This isn't the prettiest part," Possum said. "Come on!"

As he moved across the floor of the cave, the twins noticed that on the right it sloped down abruptly.

"We'll join hands now," said Possum, "so we won't slide down there. It drops to another cave about twelve feet below."

He reached back and took Nan's right hand. She put her left one behind her to grab her twin's, but did not feel it.

"Bert, where are you?"

"I—I'm sliding!" the boy cried out.

Possum swung his flashlight around. Bert was several feet from them. He was trying desperately to stop, but was heading for the drop to the other cave!

# CHAPTER XX

## THE HELPFUL "ICICLE"

"CATCH me!" Bert cried, as he started sliding faster.

Nan gave a wail of fright. Possum gasped, then said, "Sit down and dig your heels in!"

Bert did as he was told. Now the boy did not slide so fast, but still he kept going toward the dark hole to the cave below.

"Give me your belt, Nan," Possum ordered. He was pulling his own from his trousers.

Nan yanked the leather strap from her jeans. Quickly Possum buckled the two belts together and threw one end to Bert. It did not quite reach.

The bellhop gave the belt to Nan. Then he put one arm tightly around a huge, narrow rock. With the other hand he held one of Nan's wrists in a hard grip. He told her to lean toward Bert as far as she could and let the belts dangle down the slope.

*This time Bert caught hold of the strap!*

Slowly Possum pulled Nan toward him. Then he took the belt from her and drew Bert up the rest of the way. The twins were amazed at the little man's strength.

"Oh boy!" Bert cried in relief. "Thanks a lot, Possum."

"You—you saved my brother's life," said Nan.

Possum grinned and tapped the huge rock. "I guess you can thank this stalagmite," he said.

"Stal—what?" Bert asked.

The bellhop explained that the big, shining column that rose up from the floor like an upside-down ice cream cone was called a stalagmite. The "icicles" hanging down from the ceiling were stalactites. They were formed by water dripping from the roof of the cave for many hundreds of years.

"How can water make rocks?" Nan asked.

Possum said each drop of water carried sticky particles like cement. The particles stuck together, gradually building the stalactites and stalagmites.

"Well, we'd better go. Follow me," Possum ordered.

The children walked through to another room. It was even more beautiful than the first. When they spoke, their echoes came back like voices from far away under the mountain.

"Gosh," said Bert, "this place is spooky."

Possum assured the twins that there was nothing to worry about and they continued on. The ground began to rise steeply and soon the passageway became narrow.

"We haven't far to go," the bellhop said, "but you'll have to get down and crawl."

Soon they saw a patch of daylight ahead.

"Here's the end of the cave," Possum said.

He scrambled through the opening. Suddenly a harsh voice exclaimed:

"Hey, what are you doing here?"

Nan, who was ahead of Bert, peeked from the cave. A thin-faced man was sitting with his back to a tree. He had been reading a pamphlet.

"Oh!" Nan whispered to Bert. "It's Mr. Smink!"

Bert peeked out of the cave. The man got up, laid the paper on a stone, and faced Possum. When the bellhop did not answer him, Mr. Smink stood up and snapped:

"You have no right on this trail!"

"And why not?" Possum asked.

"It's—it's secret."

Bert and Nan decided to remain hidden. Maybe they would find out something more!

Possum declared the old trail did not belong to anyone. As the men continued to argue, they got farther from the cave and the tree.

"Say," said Bert to Nan, "I'll bet that paper is the one Mr. Smink stole from the library!"

"I'll bet you're right," Nan agreed. "I'll go look."

"Don't let him see you!"

Nan waited until Mr. Smink's back was turned, then she crawled from the cave. Quickly she tiptoed toward the stone where the pamphlet lay, and read the title. *The Feathered Rainbow!* It *was* the stolen pamphlet!

As the girl picked it up, she nodded to her twin. He came from the cave and stood beside Nan. Mr. Smink caught sight of the twins out of the corner of his eye. He swung around and glared at them.

"You, too!" he shouted. "Put that down!"

"It doesn't belong to you," Nan retorted.

"Is that so?" the man cried. "What gives you that idea?"

He strode over to where the children were standing and tried to snatch the paper. Nan dodged out of the way and Bert shielded her.

"You took this from the hotel library," Bert accused him. "We're going to take it back."

Mr. Smink's face grew red with anger. "You

fresh kid!" he shouted, making a lunge at Bert.

"Don't touch that boy," Possum shouted, "or you'll be sorry!"

Mr. Smink nearly had his hands on Bert, when he tripped over a vine and sprawled on his face. Bert saw his chance to learn something from Mr. Smink. He jumped on the man's back and called for the bellhop to help him. Possum held Mr. Smink's feet. The man struggled to rise, but could not budge.

"We won't let you up until you tell us what you know about the secret trail," Bert said.

"Nothing," Smink growled. "I wish I did. Now get off me! This is an outrage!" he stormed.

"Not so fast," said Possum, who realized now who the man was. "You're going to answer the children's questions!"

# CHAPTER XXI

## THE OLD CABIN

THE MAN they were holding struggled to free himself. It was no use.

"Ask him what you want to know," Possum directed the Bobbseys.

First Nan asked whether Mr. Smink had seen Mr. Lincoln since the Sportsman's Show.

"No."

"Did you follow him to the city?"

"Yes."

"And then back here?"

"Yes. He's got something that belongs to me, so I came here to get it back."

"Old Abe *is* Mr. Lincoln?" Nan asked excitedly.

Mr. Smink did not answer. Again he tried to shake off Bert and Possum. They held him tightly.

"Okay," he said finally. "Everybody calls the old man Abe, but his name's George. Now get off! That's all I know."

Nan had one more question: Where was Mr. George Lincoln's house? Smink insisted he did not know, except that it was somewhere near Rainbow Valley.

The man was released and went off glaring, across the top of the cave and out of sight. Possum grinned. He wanted to know if Bert and Nan wished to continue on the secret trail.

"Sure," Bert answered. "After we eat lunch. I'm starved."

Twenty minutes later, with the pamphlet safe in Nan's pocket, they set out. The twins trailed behind Possum as he pressed through the woods. It was hard going. If the bellhop had not been familiar with old landmarks, like a jutting rock or a gnarled oak tree, they might have lost their way.

"I haven't been over here in a long time," Possum admitted. "The woods are much denser now."

"Maybe this is where Mr. Lincoln is hiding," Bert ventured.

As the three went along, the boy kept looking for signs of footprints and ashes from campfires. Suddenly he called, "Somebody's been here!"

Possum and Nan looked where Bert was pointing. Bushes had been trampled, as if a person had broken through in a hurry.

"I'm going to see what's over there," Bert announced.

He ran ahead a few feet. Suddenly he saw something that made his heart pound fast. Ahead of him, almost hidden by big trees, stood a cabin.

"Come on!" he shouted.

Nan and Possum followed him to the log cabin. It was half tumbled down. The windows looked like big black eyes, and the door sagged out on broken hinges.

"It doesn't look as if anybody had lived here for a long time," Nan said. Possum and Bert opened the door wider and went inside. There was nothing in the room but a cot, a table, one chair, and an old stove. Beside the stove lay a few pieces of wood and a crumpled newspaper. Bert picked up the paper and gasped in astonishment.

"It's the Lakeport *Gazette!*" he exclaimed.

By this time Nan had come inside. She, too, was surprised to see the newspaper from their home town.

"Mr. Lincoln must have been here," Bert said as he looked at the date. "He got this paper while he was at the Sportsman's Show."

"It could have been Mr. Smink who left it," Nan pointed out.

They went outside. A moment later Nan ran toward one of the big trees. Around it was a broken chain.

"Kate's been here, too!" she exclaimed. "Maybe Mr. Smink had her!"

"It's sure a mystery," said Possum.

Bert asked him how much farther the secret trail went.

"Not much farther," the bellhop replied. "About a mile."

"Where does it end?"

"At Red Ridge Lodge," said Possum. "That's the spot where a tribe of Indians lived in their kind of hotel years and years ago. It was called a long house."

Possum examined the chain and declared it was hardly strong enough for a bear. Probably a dog had once been tied up there. The twins were disappointed that nothing had come of their find.

All the rest of the way along the secret trail they kept alert, looking for some sign of Mr. Lincoln, or another cabin, but saw nothing.

"I'm not going to give up till I find **it**!" Bert declared.

When they reached Red Ridge Lodge, the boy said he would go in and tell the softball captain that the Rainbow House team would be ready to play the Red Ridgers two days later. While he was gone, Danny Rugg came outside. Seeing Possum in hunter's clothes, he was curious to know what was going on. He asked Nan.

"We came to tell you about our team," Nan said. She decided not to mention the secret trail.

"Huh!" Danny replied. "You call that a team, with a girl on it?"

"How'd you know that?" Nan asked. When Danny did not answer, she said, "I suppose Gordon Bennett told you."

Danny jumped. He turned red. "My cousin talks too much," he said angrily.

Nan felt like laughing. Danny had given away a secret! Now it was clear why the two boys had been together, and why Danny was away from his hotel so late in the evening.

Instead of laughing, Nan said, "Our girl player's very good. Rainbow House is going to beat Red Ridge Lodge! And listen, Danny Rugg, you and your cousin had better not play any more jokes!"

# CHAPTER XXII

## ALONE IN THE WOODS

DANNY stared. He looked so funny that Possum burst out laughing.

"Our girl player's a champ," the bellhop said. "You want to look out for her pitching."

At this moment Bert came from the hotel. A bus was just pulling up, so he merely said, "Hello, Danny! See you Friday," and hopped aboard after Nan and Possum. When he heard that Gordon and Danny were cousins, he, too, laughed at the way Danny had given himself away.

"I'll bet he'll try something in the game to get square with us," Bert declared. He determined to watch Danny's every move.

When they reached home, Bert went at once to round up his teammates for a short practice. Next morning they would have a longer workout.

In the meantime Nan had told the other

Bobbseys and Dinah about the wonderful cave she and Bert had been in. At once Freddie and Flossie wanted to go and see it. Flossie was sure some of the fairies that came to the falls lived there.

Nan thought she could find the way to the cave, and Mr. Bobbsey said he would take them there in the morning. He also was interested to hear that Mr. Lincoln's first name was George.

"Do you think the G's on the turtle have anything to do with his name?" Nan asked her father.

Mr. Bobbsey thought probably they did, but he could not guess how, unless the second G was for a middle name. Still, it seemed strange that the woodsman had not put GGL on the turtle if those were his initials.

"I hope we find out someday," Nan sighed, and went off to feed Kate and make her do her tricks.

During the evening the children's hostess came to the Bobbsey cabin. Mrs. Nixon said that the next morning she and a young man were going to take a group of small boys and girls on a hike. Wouldn't Flossie and Freddie like to go?

"I'm sure they would," Mrs. Bobbsey told the hostess. "They were going to a cave, but they can do that another time."

"Have them bring a good lunch," Mrs. Nixon said, as she was leaving.

Flossie and Freddie were thrilled to go on the hike. Freddie thought they might even get near the cave and he could peek inside.

"How'll I know where it is?" he asked Nan just before he started for bed that night.

His sister said she had noticed a very tall tree near the cave. It had no branches except at the very top. On the trunk were lots and lots of marks —initials and pictures.

"We'll find it," said Freddie.

He was the first one up the following day, and went to the kitchen to see Dinah. She was packing a lunch, and singing. Freddie liked the song, but he could not remember the words except the first two lines:

*The bird I like best is the robin,*
*'Cause when he eats worms, he keeps bobbin'.*

Freddie began to whistle the tune, then picked up a chicken sandwich and bit into it.

"Goodness, child," said Dinah, "if you eat your lunch before you eat breakfast, I'm afraid you'll be all backwards today!"

Freddie giggled, and did not take any more of the lunch. Soon Flossie was dressed. As soon as breakfast was over, the small twins started out.

"Find the pot o' gold!" Dinah called.

The twins had been so busy that they had almost forgotten about it. Was Dinah teasing, they wondered, or was there really a treasure to be found? Freddie thought he would ask Mrs. Nixon about it.

The hostess was on the hotel porch with several boys and girls and a young man. She introduced him as Jack. While they were waiting for Helen and Billy Clark, the last two children to come, Freddie whispered to Mrs. Nixon about the pot of gold.

Flossie saw her nod her head and smile. Then Freddie and the hostess went inside the hotel. A few minutes later when they came back, Freddie was giggling. Flossie asked him why.

"It's a s'prise," he said. "You wait."

Meanwhile Helen and Billy had come, and the little group started off. Flossie walked with Helen and they began talking about their dolls. Each of them had one named Janie and each had received hers for Christmas.

"What does your dolly look like?" Flossie asked. "Is she pretty?"

"Uh-huh," Helen replied. "She—she looks like you."

After they had walked awhile, Freddie

thought it was time for the surprise, and whispered again to Mrs. Nixon.

"Pretty soon," she promised. The little boy stayed close to her side and kept feeling of something in his pocket. A few minutes later the hostess said, "How would you children like to have a treasure hunt?"

"Oh, yes."

"Please!"

"What do we hunt for?"

Mrs. Nixon told the story of how people used to think there was a pot of gold at the end of the rainbow. Nobody has ever found it because as a person walks toward a rainbow, it seems to move, and before he can reach the lovely blue and pink and yellow colors, they are gone.

Meanwhile, Freddie had walked off among the trees. He saw an old log that was just right for something to be hidden under. The little boy reached into his pocket and took out a small package. Then he leaned down and turned the log over.

"Oh!" he cried suddenly. "Go away!"

Bumblebees! Dozens of them! They flew at Freddie angrily. He backed away and ran as fast as he could. He kept on running for a long time.

When Freddie was sure the bumblebees had

been left far behind, he stopped. Suddenly he realized his little package was gone.

"Oh shucks!" he said aloud, and thought, "I can't go back and get it. The bees'll sting me sure."

Freddie knew he had spoiled the game Mrs. Nixon had planned. He had had several shiny pennies in the package. They were to be a "pot of gold" for which the other children were to hunt.

"And they're hunting right now," the little boy thought woefully. "Maybe—maybe they'll get stung!"

He decided to run back to the group as fast as he could and warn them. As he hurried, Freddie did not think about the direction he was taking. Suddenly he noticed a great pile of rocks. He had never seen them before.

"Where am I?" he asked himself, a little frightened.

Freddie looked all around. There was not a sound. The birds were having their midday nap, he decided. The squirrels and insects were quiet too. Freddie broke the stillness abruptly.

"Jack! Mrs. Nixon! Flossie!" he shouted.

Did he imagine it, or did he hear his name called from far away? He shouted again, then listened.

"I did hear it," he declared, and started running toward the sound.

To his amazement he saw Flossie sitting on a rock. She had been crying.

"Where you been?" she asked Freddie.

He told her, and said they must hurry back. His twin shook her head. She had hurt her leg, and could not go fast.

"I saw you run away," she said, "so I ran, too. And then I couldn't see you any more, but I could hear you. When I fell down, I couldn't go after you any more."

Freddie offered to find the others and come back for her. But Flossie would not hear of this. She stood up and declared her bruised leg felt better.

The little twins started off. Presently they saw a very large tree trunk with all sorts of marks on it.

"Hey," said Freddie, stopping, "this might be the tree Nan told us about."

"You mean the one near the cave?" Flossie asked.

"Sure."

Freddie began to look for the cave. It was not many minutes before he found the opening and called Flossie.

"Don't go in," she warned.

"Why not?"

"It's—it's dark and slippery," said Flossie.

"I'll just go in a little way," her twin promised.

By the time Freddie had crawled in five feet, he had had enough. He could not see a thing. The little boy backed out hurriedly.

"If I'd had a flashlight, I wouldn't have come out," he boasted.

Flossie was relieved. "Come on," she said, "it's going to rain."

The sunshine was gone. It was very gloomy in the woods. The wind was whipping the leaves, and it had grown quite chilly. Flossie shivered a little.

The twins trudged along. Each one thought the other knew the way to the spot where Jack and Mrs. Nixon and the other children had been. Presently Flossie said, "It's awful far, Freddie. Are you sure you know where you're going?"

The little boy stopped and looked at her. "I thought you knew," he said.

Then the same dreadful thought came to the small twins. They were lost in the great woods on Rainbow Mountain!

# CHAPTER XXIII

NOT KNOWING what else to do, Freddie and Flossie turned back toward the cave. At least they could crawl inside it until the rain was over.

"Nan'll know where we are," said Flossie hopefully as they hurried along. But after they had walked for ten minutes, and had not come to the cave, the children knew they had taken the wrong direction.

"Oh dear," said Flossie, "every way we go is the wrong way."

A few drops of rain fell among the trees and splashed on the twins' faces. They looked around for something under which to crawl. There were no overhanging rocks or hollow trees.

"What'll we do?" Flossie asked, becoming frightened.

"Don't worry, Flossie," Freddie said manfully. "We'll build a lean-to."

Flossie liked the idea, but she was sure they were not big enough to make one like the one Mr. Lincoln had built at the Sportsman's Show. She remembered that he had started by using vines to tie a long pole between two trees.

"There aren't any vines around here," she told Freddie.

The little boy thought hard. How could they make the pole stay up? His bright eyes spied two old trees standing about five steps apart, with branches very near the ground; in fact, they were not much higher than the twins' heads.

"Come on!" he said to his sister. "Help me find a pole, and we'd better hurry. It's raining harder now."

Flossie was the one who found a long slender sapling which had been broken off. Perhaps someone had planned to use it, and changed his mind.

Freddie took hold of one end and Flossie the other. They carried the sapling to the old trees. It was hard work lifting it up to the crotches of the trees, but finally they succeeded.

"Now we have to find something for the side of our house," said Flossie. "Oh dear, I'm getting wet."

Freddie already was picking up a long piece of bark. This would do nicely for one section of the lean-to. While he was setting it in place at a slant, Flossie ran over to a fallen branch. The thick leaves were still on it. She asked Freddie to come and help lift it. In a minute they stood it at an angle beside the bark.

There was still some to be covered. The twins scurried around trying to find something that would do. The rain was falling faster now and the wind was blowing harder. Suddenly the piece of bark blew down.

Flossie and Freddie were on the verge of tears, but they would not give up. They set the bark in place again and rolled a stone up against it. But it blew down a moment later.

"I know what's the matter," said Freddie. "We have to fix it so the wind'll blow on the back of our house."

The two children carried the bark and the tree branch to the other side of the cross pole and set them up. This time the wind held them tight against it.

As the children stepped back to be sure their work was all right, Freddie kicked something on the ground. Looking down, he saw an old sack. Some camper must have left it there. The sack was very dirty but it would serve their purpose nicely, Freddie decided.

Flossie found two long sticks and put them

inside the two corners of the sack. Then the children raised them up against the pole.

The lean-to was finished! And not a moment too soon. The rain started to pelt down hard.

The twins crawled under their little shelter. It was very cozy. The rain and the wind beat on the back of it but only a few drops came through. Fortunately the ground sloped down from the front of the lean-to, so the rain did not run inside.

At first Freddie and Flossie thought it was like playing house a new way. But after a while they grew tired of the game. It was still raining, and suddenly they remembered all over again that they were lost in the woods.

The two children became very quiet. Each was trying to be brave and not cry. Presently their eyes closed. The small twins fell asleep.

Freddie was the first one to awaken. For a moment he did not know where he was. As he sat up to get a better look, he jostled Flossie. She, too, sat up. There was just a little daylight left.

"Oh, Freddie," she said, "it's almost nighttime."

"Maybe it's almost morning," her twin said. "I'm awful hungry."

Flossie was not thinking about being hungry. All she wanted was to see her mother and daddy.

"Listen!" Freddie said suddenly. "Somebody's coming."

He was sure it must be his parents. The twins got up and went outside. Freddie was just about to shout, "Here we are!" when they heard angry voices. These could not be rescuers, he decided.

The children peered out through the dusk. They could see two men coming toward them. Flossie clutched Freddie's hand. She heard one of the men say:

"Listen here, Smink, you find that kid or you'll be sorry!"

"I've told you a hundred times," Mr. Smink replied, "I don't know where he is."

"Is that so?" said the other man. "Well, I'll give you just two more days to find Georgie Grant. Now get moving."

He took some money from his pocket and tossed it to Mr. Smink. Then the two men started off. They had not gone far when Freddie said excitedly to his sister, "Let's follow them!"

"But they might see us," Flossie objected.

"We can be real quiet," Freddie suggested. "And don't you see, they may lead us back to Rainbow House."

"All right," Flossie agreed.

The twins started off on tiptoe.

# CHAPTER XXIV

## THE SECRET PATH

"IT MUST be night," said Flossie, as the twins went along after Mr. Smink and his friend.

It was getting darker each minute, and the children could barely see the two men. And they walked so fast that Flossie and Freddie found it necessary to run a good part of the time. Suddenly the men disappeared completely.

"Oh, what will we do?" Flossie exclaimed.

"I see a light," said Freddie cheerfully.

Since the light did not move, he decided it must be in a house. Hoping that the people who lived in the house would be friendly, the twins went up and rapped on the door. It was opened by a woman with a very kind face.

"Well, for goodness sake," she said, "where did you children come from?"

"We're lost," said Freddie. "Please take us home. We're two of the Bobbsey twins."

"Two of the Bobbsey twins? How many of you are there?" the woman asked.

Flossie answered this time and said there were four of them and that they lived in a cabin near Rainbow House. She also told how she and Freddie had become separated from the other young hikers.

The woman invited the children inside and said her husband would take them home as soon as he came in. He should be back in a few minutes from an errand. While they were waiting, she made some sandwiches and poured out two glasses of milk. How good they tasted to Freddie and Flossie!

Just as the twins finished eating, the woman's husband came home. He said he would gladly take the children to their parents. Actually, they were not very far from Rainbow House.

He got a lantern and two flashlights. After giving a flashlight to each child, the man said, "We're ready to go."

They talked little on the way home, but Freddie did ask the man if he knew a boy named Georgie Grant, or a woodsman named Mr. Lincoln, or a bad man named Mr. Smink.

"I've never heard of any of them," the man answered, so the children said no more about them.

In twenty minutes they reached Rainbow
House. There was a big crowd of people outside. When they saw Flossie and Freddie, several
of them ran to meet the twins.

"Where have you been?"

"Your parents are frightened to death.
They're out looking for you now."

"We must ring the bell," said one man.

Freddie and Flossie asked why. They were
told that many people were out in the woods
searching for the children. It had been arranged
that if anyone found them, they were to telephone to the town firehouse and the big fire bell
would be rung. Then the searchers would come
home.

Flossie and Freddie were sorry they had
caused so much trouble, and a little bit nervous
about what their mother and daddy might say.

Flossie turned around to speak to the man who
had brought them home, but he had gone. A moment later a bell in the distance began to ring.

"That should bring everyone home," said one
of the men. "Come now, Freddie and Flossie,
I'll take you down to your cabin. I guess Dinah
will be relieved to see you, too."

Indeed Dinah was relieved to see them. For
the first time Flossie and Freddie found out what
time it was and what day it was. Actually they

had slept only a few hours. It was still Thursday and it was only ten o'clock.

Dinah had to hear the whole story of their adventure. She did not mention bed, but the little twins could not keep their eyes open. So finally she helped them undress and tucked them in.

When their worried parents and Bert and Nan arrived, it was Dinah who retold the story, because Freddie and Flossie were sound asleep. When she got to the part about Georgie Grant, Nan and Bert became very much excited.

"Why, those are the initials on the turtle we found!" Bert exclaimed. "The one Mr. Lincoln said he put into the water. G. G. must be Georgie Grant's initials."

A thought came to Nan. Georgie Grant must be living with Mr. Lincoln! But why were they hiding? And what did Mr. Smink have to do with it? Nobody could figure this out.

When the small twins awoke next morning, they received especially big hugs from their mother and father and Nan. Bert was not there to tell them how glad he was that they were back safely. He had already gone up to the hotel to meet his friends on the softball team.

This was the day of the big game against the Red Ridge Lodge team. At this very moment

Captain Bert Bobbsey was saying to the other boys and Sarah:

"Most of those Red Ridgers are swell fellows, but one of them might try something tricky, so watch your step."

On purpose he did not mention Danny Rugg's name because his cousin Gordon Bennett was still on the Rainbow House team.

The players had a little batting practice and Sarah pitched a few balls, then all the group went off for an early lunch.

At two o'clock a large bus rolled up in front of Rainbow House with the Red Ridgers and their coach. Parents, brothers, sisters, and other guests followed in their own cars. Practically everyone at the Lodge had come over to see the game.

They were met by a welcoming cheer from Rainbow House rooters. As the players piled out of the bus, Danny spied Gordon and ran over to him.

"What's eating you?" Danny said to his sour-looking cousin.

"Jack won't let me pitch," Gordon mumbled, "but I've got an idea. If our team starts winning, I'm not going to let Bert Bobbsey hog all the glory. I'll drop a couple of fly balls, that's what!"

"You won't even have to do that," Danny snickered. "I've got a better plan." He put one arm around his cousin's shoulder and led him aside, whispering in his ear.

Soon the players took their positions on the field, the umpire shouted, "Play ball!" and the first Red Ridger swung his bat at home plate. Sarah pitched well, but so did the visiting pitcher. At the end of the third inning nobody had scored.

In the fourth inning things began to happen. Bert hit the ball a good whack into the outfield. The center fielder picked it up and threw to second base, where Danny was playing. Bert raced past first and slid into second in a cloud of dust.

A second later as Danny touched him with the ball, he landed with both feet on Bert's right foot. Bert winced with pain, but got up and brushed himself off. He was sure Danny had done it deliberately, but Bert would not let him know he had been hurt.

"Hooray for Bert's two-bagger!" the rooters shouted, as the umpire called him safe.

Sarah was up next. She hit the ball toward Danny and started for first. He scooped it up and threw toward the baseman. But the ball seemed to go wild and hit the girl hard on the left arm.

"You did that on purpose," the umpire cried out. "Sarah is safe on first."

Bert, meanwhile, had run to third base. When he saw Sarah rubbing her arm, he called time out.

"Oh, we've lost our pitcher," groaned one of the Rainbow rooters.

"I can use my other arm," the girl replied defiantly.

Nobody had dreamed Sarah could pitch with her right arm, too! As the game went on, though, she proved it, as she struck out batter after batter.

The other Rainbow players were so angry at Danny's lack of sportsmanship that they hit the ball with all their might. In the fifth inning Bert got another double, and in the sixth he slammed a home run in spite of his injured foot. When the game finally was over, Freddie Bobbsey screamed excitedly:

"We won! We won!"

Bert and the other boys were slapped on the back, and many grownups came to shake Sarah's hand for her ten-to-two victory.

As the last of the cheering died away, Captain Bert Bobbsey started for home. His foot was paining him badly. Still he did not want anyone to know about it. "I'll just go down by the falls and soak my foot in that nice cold water," he told himself.

The only person who saw him go was Nan. She ran after him to find out what was the matter.

When they reached the falls, Bert took off his shoe and sock and dipped his swollen foot in the water. How soothing its coolness was!

The twins had been there about five minutes when they heard the strange singing that seemed to come out of the waterfall. As they listened intently, Nan suddenly grabbed her brother's arm.

"Bert!" she gasped. "I just saw—I just saw Mr. Lincoln! He went right behind the waterfall!"

Like a deer, Nan jumped up and leaped to the edge of the waterfall. She caught a glimpse of the old woodsman a little distance ahead, right behind the curtain of thundering water.

Nan realized that the dangerous ledge of rock back of the water must be a secret trail. Did she dare follow the woodsman along that trail?

# CHAPTER XXV

## HAPPY CHILDREN

NAN DECIDED to follow Mr. Lincoln. Signaling to Bert, she disappeared behind the waterfall.

Quickly Bert Bobbsey put on his shoe and dashed to the rock ledge. Nan and the woodsman were nearly out of sight.

As he came to the far side of the falls, Bert was amazed to see misty stone steps leading upward. His twin was at the top and he scrambled up after her.

Meanwhile Nan had hurried through the dense woods at the top of the falls after the old woodsman. She finally succeeded in catching up to him and called out:

"Mr. Lincoln! Mr. Lincoln! Wait for me!"

The old man turned around. He seemed completely stunned to see Nan Bobbsey.

"My secret trail!" he cried out. "How did you find it?"

Nan told him how she and Bert had tried for days and days to locate him. First they had wanted to return his knife. Then they had found Kate and wondered if he wanted her back.

"No, no," Mr. Lincoln replied. "And you must not come any farther. I will take you back under the falls, and you must never come here again."

"But why?" Nan asked. "Is it because of Georgie Grant?"

Mr. Lincoln stared at her so hard that Nan Bobbsey became a little frightened. Just then she heard a noise in the woods and turned her head. Bert was just appearing among the trees. As the boy came up Mr. Lincoln asked:

"When did you children hear about Georgie Grant?"

Nan told how the Bobbseys had pieced out the puzzle of the initials on the turtle after Flossie and Freddie had heard Mr. Smink mention Georgie Grant's name. She said Mr. Smink and a friend of his had been trying for a long time to find Mr. Lincoln. The old woodsman's face became very grave.

"Since you children were able to find me, no doubt Smink will, too. And then he'll take Georgie away from me," he added sadly.

"Who is Georgie?" Nan asked.

"My grandson."

Mr. Lincoln told the twins that his ten-year-old grandson had a beautiful singing voice. The twins said they had heard it. The woodsman was surprised to learn that the voice had carried above the roar of the water.

"When Georgie's parents died," he explained, "Mr. Smink was appointed his guardian. I wanted Georgie with me, but everyone thought his voice should be trained, so he was kept in the city.

"But Mr. Smink is a wicked man. He used Georgie's money for himself, and made the boy sing in places not fit for a child.

"Georgie finally wrote a letter to me at Westbrook. I didn't pick it up until I was on my way to the Sportsman's Show. Then I went to the city. I found Georgie alone, and brought him back here."

"Is this where you've always lived?" Nan asked the woodsman.

Mr. Lincoln said he had found the secret spot years before while on a vacation from the city. He had never told anyone about it. Whenever he wanted to be alone, he came to stay in the cabin he had built. He figured Indians long ago had carved out the stone steps.

"I thought it was a fine hideout for Georgie

and me," he said, "but now I'm afraid Smink will come."

"Maybe my dad can help you," Bert spoke up.

Mr. Lincoln thought this was a good suggestion, and asked the twins to return home and tell his story. He said his cabin was only a short distance ahead, though, and suggested that they come and meet Georgie before going back.

On the way Nan asked whether Mr. Lincoln was the mysterious ghost who had left baskets and asked for food in return. The old woodsman said he was.

"It was the only way I could think of to get supplies without anyone seeing me. Once I almost got caught by some boy, so I went to another locality and left my baskets and notes."

Bert grinned and said he had been that boy. "Do you use a light at night when you go back of the falls?" Bert asked him.

"Yes, I have to."

"Then that's what I saw," said Bert. "Gosh, I sure was scared!"

By this time they had reached the old man's attractive little cabin. A handsome boy rushed outside. When he saw the twins, he turned quickly and ran, but his grandfather called out that it was perfectly safe for him to come back.

He introduced his grandson and explained

who the Bobbseys were. Perhaps their father
could help to straighten out the tangle about Mr.
Smink, he told Georgie.

"Oh, that would make Grandpop and me
happy," said Georgie wistfully.

"We'd better go now," Nan spoke up. "Bert
and I will let you know right away what hap-
pens."

The twins got about halfway to the falls
when suddenly they saw two men coming toward
them. To their utter dismay the children realized they were Mr. Smink and his friend!

"Oh!" said Nan in fright. "They mustn't take
Georgie Grant!"

"We'd better run back and warn Mr. Lincoln!" Bert exclaimed.

The twins raced to the cabin and told Georgie
and his grandfather about the two men. Mr. Lincoln and Georgie were in despair.

"I know!" cried Bert. "Mr. Lincoln, let
Georgie come with Nan and me! He can stay at
our house and Mr. Smink won't know where he
is."

"Yes, yes, do that," said Mr. Lincoln hurriedly, "but don't let those men see you."

The three children hurried outside. Georgie
took them by another secret trail to the waterfall, so they escaped the boy's guardian and his

friend. Carefully the children made their way down the slippery stone steps and along the rock ledge back of the waterfall.

Bert led the way to the Bobbsey cabin. The twins introduced Georgie to the rest of the family and quickly told what had happened.

"Dad," said Nan, "you can help Georgie right away, can't you?"

Mr. Bobbsey said that, fortunately, one of the hotel guests was a judge, who could tell them exactly what to do. He went up to the hotel at once to speak to the judge. The conversation was a long one, and all the children fidgeted while waiting to find out what was going to happen to Georgie. Finally Mr. Bobbsey returned.

"I have good news for you, Georgie," he said kindly. "Judge Jones says a new guardian can be appointed for you, and you can have your singing lessons."

"But Mr. Smink used up all my money," Georgie said. "Maybe it would be better if I just stayed with my grandfather."

The minute Nan heard this, she began to think what might be done to get some money for Georgie's singing lessons. Presently an idea popped into her head. She asked to be excused and ran as fast as she could up to the hotel and went straight to Mrs. Nixon. After telling Georgie's story, she asked:

"Do you think the hotel would let him give a concert, and would all the people at Rainbow House pay to hear him sing?"

Mrs. Nixon's eyes sparkled. "I'm sure they would," she answered, "and I think we can do even better than that. I believe all the summer guests in the hotels of Rainbow Valley and the mountains around here would like to hear a fine boy soprano. I'll start making arrangements at once."

How happily everything was turning out! Judge Jones had notified the State Troopers about Mr. Smink and his friend. The officers had come at once to Mr. Lincoln's cabin and ordered the two men to stay away from Georgie.

It was learned that they had seen Bert disappearing behind the waterfall, and in this way had found the secret trail for which they had been looking.

The evening of Georgie's concert arrived. So many tickets had been sold that the affair had to be held on the play field of Rainbow House. There would be hundreds of dollars toward Georgie Grant's music lessons. The Bobbsey twins were given full credit for their part in solving the mystery and finding the boy soprano.

Georgie sang beautifully and with each number the applause became more enthusiastic. When the concert was over, a woman came to old Mr. Lincoln and said she was a singing teacher from New York City. She would like very much to give free lessons to Georgie Grant.

"Although," she smiled, "the boy has such a beautiful natural voice that he will not need much training. He will be ready in a short time to be a church soloist and earn his own living."

Everyone else wanted to meet Georgie, but finally Mr. Lincoln felt that he should go home and rest. On the way, both the boy and his grandfather stopped in for a few minutes at the Bobbsey cabin.

When the elderly woodsman tried to thank the Bobbseys, the twins' mother said they had done little enough in return for Mr. Lincoln's having rescued Freddie from the river.

Flossie and Freddie insisted upon holding Georgie's hands as they went down the path together. Presently Flossie looked up at him and said, "All the mysteries are solved 'cept one. Why did your bear Kate run away?"

Georgie answered, chuckling, "Because she can't bear to hear me sing!"

Could anything be more fun than having a real little train of your own? **THE BOBBSEY TWINS** have one, and when they ride on it they have all sorts of adventures along the way.

Be sure to read

# THE BOBBSEY TWINS' OWN LITTLE RAILROAD.